I0824882

HURON BLACKHEART

MASTER OF THE MAELSTROM

By the same author

THE LION: SON OF THE FOREST

• SOLOMON AKURRA •
HARROWMASTER
GHOST LEGION

ALPHARIUS: HEAD OF THE HYDRA
A Horus Heresy Primarchs novel

RITES OF PASSAGE
A Navis Nobilite novel

BRUTAL KUNNIN
An orks novel

DA GOBBO'S REVENGE
An orks novella

ROAD TO REDEMPTION
A Necromunda novel

WANTED: DEAD
A Necromunda novella

More Chaos Space Marines from Black Library

• BLACK LEGION •
by Aaron Dembski-Bowden
BOOK 1: *The Talon of Horus*
BOOK 2: *Black Legion*

• AHRIMAN •
by John French
BOOK 1: *Exile*
BOOK 2: *Sorcerer*
BOOK 3: *Unchanged*
BOOK 4: *Eternal*
BOOK 5: *Undying*

• FABIUS BILE •
by Josh Reynolds
BOOK 1: *Primogenitor*
BOOK 2: *Clonelord*
BOOK 3: *Manflayer*

NIGHT LORDS: THE OMNIBUS
An omnibus edition of the novels *Soul Hunter*, *Blood Reaver* and *Void Stalker* by Aaron Dembski-Bowden

HURON BLACKHEART
MASTER OF THE MAELSTROM

MIKE BROOKS

BLACK LIBRARY

A BLACK LIBRARY PUBLICATION

First published in 2022.
This edition published in Great Britain in 2026 by
Black Library, Games Workshop Ltd., Willow Road,
Nottingham, NG7 2WS, UK.

Represented by: Games Workshop Limited – Irish branch,
Unit 3, Lower Liffey Street, Dublin 1,
D01 K199, Ireland.

10 9 8 7 6 5 4 3 2 1

Produced by Games Workshop in Nottingham.
Cover illustration by Jake Murray.

Huron Blackheart: Master of the Maelstrom © Copyright Games Workshop Limited 2026. Huron Blackheart: Master of the Maelstrom, GW, Games Workshop, Black Library, The Horus Heresy, The Horus Heresy Eye logo, Space Marine, 40K, Warhammer, Warhammer 40,000, the 'Aquila' Double-headed Eagle logo, and all associated logos, illustrations, images, names, creatures, races, vehicles, locations, weapons, characters, and the distinctive likenesses thereof, are either ® or TM, and/or © Games Workshop Limited, variably registered around the world.
All Rights Reserved.

A CIP record for this book is available from the British Library.

ISBN 13: 978-1-83609-272-8

No part of this publication may be reproduced, stored in a retrieval system, or transmitted in any form or by any means, electronic, mechanical, photocopying, recording or otherwise, without the prior permission of the publishers.

This is a work of fiction. All the characters and events portrayed in this book are fictional, and any resemblance to real people or incidents is purely coincidental.

See Black Library on the internet at

blacklibrary.com

Find out more about Games Workshop and the world of Warhammer 40,000 at

games-workshop.com

Printed and bound in the UK.

For my Necromunda campaign group, in thanks for all these years of treachery, bloodshed and genestealers in unfeasibly small boxes.

For more than a hundred centuries the Emperor has sat immobile on the Golden Throne of Earth. He is the Master of Mankind. By the might of his inexhaustible armies a million worlds stand against the dark.

Yet, he is a rotting carcass, the Carrion Lord of the Imperium held in life by marvels from the Dark Age of Technology and the thousand souls sacrificed each day so his may continue to burn.

To be a man in such times is to be one amongst untold billions. It is to live in the cruelest and most bloody regime imaginable. It is to suffer an eternity of carnage and slaughter. It is to have cries of anguish and sorrow drowned by the thirsting laughter of dark gods.

This is a dark and terrible era where you will find little comfort or hope. Forget the power of technology and science. Forget the promise of progress and advancement. Forget any notion of common humanity or compassion.

There is no peace amongst the stars, for in the grim darkness of the far future, there is only war.

When I with fearful eye did see
Approaching o'er the mountain's crest
The bloody-handed fiend we sought
My heart did still within my chest

In us, dark hubris had been wrought
To think that we could bring him down
For he let loose with laughter's peal
And mountains trembled at the sound

I gazed upon his fierce visage
His taloned arms now spread out wide
And felt my soul shrink from him as
He bid us join him at his side

– Extract from *The Lament of Tuomas Pridefall*,
by Eudaris Settler

PROLOGUE

'Force Captain!'

Captain Julius Katra of the Ultramarines turns towards the hail. He is the commander of Task Force XXV of the Kallides battle group, part of the Indomitus Crusade in Roboute Guilliman's own Fleet Primus. He has been tasked with bringing the light of the Imperium back to the galaxy, one world at a time if needs be, and the ships and troops under his command are eager for more battle. The Avenging Son has returned, and he is blazing a trail across the stars such as has not been seen since the Great Crusade itself, ten thousand years ago.

The figure making its way across the bridge of the *Light of Honour* is not an Ultramarine, however: it is human, wizened, and leaning on a staff for support. Julius frowns at the sight.

'Madame Sethica? What is amiss?'

The chief astropath turns her blind eyes towards him. 'I wanted to come myself, captain. The choir is agitated. We have received...' She shudders. 'These have been troubled times, that goes without saying, but I fear I must report a new threat to you.'

Julius nods, unperturbed. Without threat, he has no purpose. 'Please proceed.'

'I shall give you the contents of the message first,' Sethica replies, 'so that you may make your own interpretation before I give you ours. We saw a blood-red figure striding the stars, with a cruel black claw for its right hand.'

'Abaddon?' Julius asks. Sethica's lips tighten at the interruption.

'I do not believe so, Force Captain. The... *impression*, if you will, is different to the times when references to the Despoiler have blighted our vision. The figure shifts and blurs as a shining warrior approaches, and the shining one can never land a telling blow. Then there were images of a world I do not recognise, but associated with it was a skull, and a star, and a sword piercing a moon. The red figure's claw reaches out to crush this world.'

'An attack on an Imperial planet,' Julius says. 'That much seems clear. A distress call?'

'Perhaps,' Sethica replies. 'But although it is hard to put into words, the sensation of the message was not of a cry for help, but of a warning. We feel this event has not yet come to pass – perhaps it is from someone who has learned of an enemy's intentions, and wishes us to be ready.'

'You could not identify the source?'

Sethica shakes her head. 'The message was strongly laced with anger, and above all with pain, but I cannot tell you who sent it.'

Julius considers. Space Marines are not widely known for their abstract thinking, or their grasp of metaphor, being rather more concerned with the practical matters of war. However, when a soul lacks poetical understanding, an eidetic memory can sometimes fill the gaps.

'I believe I can identify a world that has some association with the symbols you have mentioned,' he says slowly. 'As for the aggressor, that is less clear to me.'

'I can give you nothing more from the vision we received,' Sethica tells him, 'but I think I can assist with my own insight. You see, Force Captain, I was born on Badab Primaris…'

ONE

Blood flows.

Not in veins, where evolution has dictated that it should, but over metal decking pitted with the gradual ravages of oxidisation that no amount of care could prevent. It dribbles down walls, from where it arced after being brutally released from its fleshy prison. It seeps into cracks and crevices. It pools in slight depressions, and drips through gratings to drizzle onto whatever lies beneath. The metallic tang of it is everywhere, mixing with the stink of burned hair, the chemical reek of promethium fumes, the sharp scent of cordite, and hints of ozone as the charged blades of power weapons gradually fuse the atoms of the air.

And through the blood comes the Blood Reaver.

Once, Lugft Huron was the Chapter Master of the Astral Claws. Once, he was a towering Space Marine warrior, the galaxy's image of nobility and righteousness: at least, to those parts of the galaxy that cowered behind the shield his warriors made from their bodies, and their guns, and their will. Once, Huron believed in the Imperium, and in the Emperor, and in his Chapter's duties: at least in his own way.

But in the Imperium there is little tolerance for any way other than that which the Imperium itself dictates. The tool that does not completely fit its role is eliminated; and if, like Lugft Huron, the tool is too tough and too stubborn to be properly eliminated, it is cast out.

The problem with that, of course, is that those who are cast out can come back. And when they do, their bodies and their guns and their will are no longer a shield, but a sword aimed for the heart.

Huron Blackheart looks around and sees death: not just death, but slaughter. This is not a military outpost; not an Astra Militarum barracks, an Adeptus Astartes fortress-monastery, or a convent of the Adepta Sororitas. This is Adeptus Mechanicus mining station Delta-Kappa-39006, plundering the mineral resources of an asteroid with a diameter of roughly three hundred miles, and its defences have been easily overwhelmed. The ships tasked with its protection were annihilated by the *Spectre of Ruin* within moments of its exit from the warp, and the Red Corsairs have overrun the station itself. Huron could have targeted the astropath's tower, to ensure that the station could not call for help, but he has not cared enough to do so.

Let the blind psykers scream. Abaddon the Despoiler has ripped the galaxy apart, and the Imperium has far greater matters to attend to. No one is coming here.

'Progress?' Huron rasps. His voice is as damaged as the rest of him. What was once a commanding basso boom is now a phlegm-edged rattle. Sometimes it betrays him altogether, until his underlings can coax his half-dead flesh back into synergy with the mechanical implants that allow him some measure of control over his own body. These are souvenirs of events in the Palace of Thorns: a reminder of how the Imperium treats its own when they dare question an unfair system.

Still, damaged or not, Huron's voice is acknowledged and obeyed just as fast as it ever was. Perhaps faster.

'We've taken most of the complex, lord,' a man replies, dropping to one knee, heedless of the bloody remains of a Mechanicus defender within inches of his leg.

The man is wearing a uniform that once belonged to a member of the Mordian Iron Guard, now with the aquila torn off and the epaulettes replaced by loyalist skulls. Perhaps he is its original owner. The Red Corsairs are a warband: the strong core of it is made up of renegade Space Marines, both from the old Astral Claws and those of other Chapters who have traded their former colours in for Huron's, but great numbers of mortal warriors have also flocked to his banner over the decades. Huron welcomes all those who will fight in his name; or at least those who do so well.

'"Most"?' he repeats, and the ragged team of men and women stiffen. There are a dozen or so of them, armed with lasguns and autoguns, and Huron could tear through them all in a matter of seconds. They know this.

'One part holds out, lord,' the kneeling man says hoarsely. Perhaps he fears that Huron's power axe will take his head, or the Tyrant's Claw will envelop him in its crackling fingers and crush the life from him, or Huron will trigger the heavy flamer embedded in the palm of that power gauntlet and simply roast him alive. 'There is only one access corridor, and the defenders are fiercer than we anticipated – combat automata, at least three of them.' He begins to speak faster, perhaps hoping to head off the displeasure of the renegade standing over him. 'If the lords of your brethren were willing, I'm sure they could attack that part of the complex from the outside, but we lack void suits and so–'

'Enough.' Huron cuts him off with a dismissive wave of fingers from the Tyrant's Claw, and the man falls silent. Huron can hear his heart pounding, can see the pulse of the vein in his neck as his blood courses through him. Human blood, mortal blood; so very different from that which cycles through Huron's twin hearts, and yet the basis for it.

Or so Huron presumes. He has been in the Maelstrom for years now, in that rift where the warp bleeds through and has its way with realspace. There is no predicting how the warp will change you: it defies logic, defies science, defies reason. The man kneeling in front of him, in fear of his life, may have already been altered. Perhaps his blood is no longer human, either. He came to the Red Corsairs as a weak mortal, the sort of malleable clay the warp can twist without effort.

Those possessed of a stronger will, on the other hand, can be harder to change; and there are few beings in the galaxy with a will stronger than that of Huron Blackheart. Most warriors, even those of the Adeptus Astartes, would have succumbed to the injuries he took in the retreat from the Palace of Thorns, rather than live on as he has. Part of that is due to a potent mix of spite and his indomitable spirit. Part of that is due to the skill of his loyal warriors Armenneus Valthex and Lord Apothecary Garreon, who worked to save him when he lay wounded. And part of that is because of the bargain Huron has struck.

He can feel a part of that bargain patrolling back and forth on his shoulders. The Hamadrya chitters softly as it phases into visibility, and the kneeling man looks up at the sound, then blanches and lowers his eyes again quickly. Huron finds the contrast amusing. A towering, horrifically scarred transhuman warrior in blood-red armour plate, wielding weapons of fearsome potency, is to be feared and obeyed; yet his daemonic familiar, a creature no larger than a domestic felid, is too unnerving to even look upon.

'Combat automata?' Huron asks, turning the words over in his mouth.

The Legio Cybernetica are formidable foes indeed; at least when they have a datasmith to update their command protocols, and adapt them to changing situations. A headlong rush into their guns will serve little purpose other than to amass skulls for the Blood God, and Huron prefers those sacrifices to be offered in scenarios where they will materially benefit him. He has brought a small number of Heretic Space Marines with him for this strike, oath-bonded killers with centuries of combined experience in bloodshed, and they could indeed approach over the asteroid's surface and breach the last part of the complex from the outside. However, he is not certain he is willing to risk them on such an assault. Such is the weight of command, for Huron has no superior. Even as a Chapter Master of the Imperium, and supposedly the sovereign commander of the Astral Claws, he was expected to respond to the 'requests' made of him for aid. As Master of the Maelstrom, he has no orders to carry out save his own. There is no hiding place, should his strategies falter.

Perhaps another approach can be attempted.

'Where is the start of this killing ground?' he demands.

There is a pile of burned and pulverised bodies outside a pair of blast doors, and they bear the ragtag motley of the mortal warriors of Huron's raiders, rather than the red robes of the defenders. The Mechanicus sigils over the door mean nothing to Huron, and he does not bother to call for any of the heretek priests who have accompanied his force on this raid to translate for him. Instead he simply presses the release, and steps to one side.

A roaring barrage of fire is the immediate response, as the incandescent fury of heavy phosphor blasters rips into the already half-melted bulkhead opposite. Huron keys the pad to keep the door open, and waits. After three seconds, the shooting stops, leaving the wall glowing.

'Impressive,' Huron rasps, pitching his voice to carry over the faint pinking of cooling metal. 'To whom am I speaking?'

There is no reply from beyond the hatch. Huron listens intently. Kastelan battle robots, unless he misses his guess: mighty automata perhaps twice as tall as he is, ferociously tough and very well armed. If he hears them coming for him, he will have to be ready to react at a moment's notice. There is presumably a reason they are holding this ground, though, instead of coming out to try and repel his force's intrusion into the complex as a whole. Perhaps they will stay put for now.

There is still no reply.

'Nothing to say?' Huron asks the silent hatchway. No, not quite silent: if he strains his hearing, he can just make out the very faint buzz of the machinery and circuits of the warrior automata, although it is barely audible over the sound of his own armour. 'You have just tried to kill me – do you not wish to know who I am?'

He closes his eyes, and reaches out with his senses. On his shoulder, the Hamadrya chitters a babble of quiet syllables that come close to being words, but which never quite develop that far. They ease his mind loose, allowing part of it to quest out in search of answers.

Blunt shapes, present and whole, entirely free from the spark of life, and yet animate. The kastelans: five of them, arrayed across the corridor. Huron can feel the belligerent energy of their machine-spirits, well suited to the task to which they have been set. And behind them...

'*There* you are,' the Blood Reaver whispers to himself, his dead lips twisting into a smile.

Behind them is true life. One soul only, about whom fear hangs as thick and obvious as captured banners on the walls of a warlord's hall. Fearful, yes, but also resolute of purpose. If it is just a labourer taking shelter behind these guards then there is no way through that will not claim a high price in blood; perhaps higher than Huron is willing to pay for such uncertain reward. If, however, it is the Legio Cybernetica datasmith – the one who controls the kastelans – then another approach is possible, and Huron has always been one to keep his options open. The commander who leashes themselves too firmly to a course of action is the one who will find themselves led by it, and not the other way around.

'A formidable force you have there,' he says. 'Too formidable to leave intact to serve the Imperium. Even now, my warriors are tearing this complex apart to secure the materials we came for. When we are done, I will have my ship level it. We have the weapons and the precision to achieve it, believe me.'

Still no response. No words, no attack. However, Huron can sense fear surging higher. Whoever this is, they have not progressed far enough down the path of the Machine Cult to eliminate all their emotions.

'I am Huron Blackheart, master of the Red Corsairs,' Huron says conversationally. 'Who is it who has stalled me so?'

Still nothing. Until–

'Cybernetica Datasmith Griza Dallax,' comes the reply, the

words tinged with both fear and pride. 'I command these machines, so do your worst.'

'My worst?' Huron gives a breathy chuckle. 'My worst would see you reduced to your component atoms as your existence catches fire around you. Have you ever died, Magos Dallax? I have, or as close to it as makes no difference. Let me tell you that your last instants are stretched out into a subjective eternity. I came out the other side. I am not certain you would be so fortunate.'

Silence.

'And what of your charges?' Huron continues. 'Valuable servants of the Omnissiah, all of them. Can they withstand an orbital bombardment? I doubt it. I am a practical man, and I detest waste. Perhaps I can offer an alternative.'

Magos Dallax does not reply, but Huron can practically taste the desperation on the air. He knows the emotion well. Dallax might stand alongside her kastelans and fight and die with them in the teeth of an attack, but to stand quietly and wait for obliteration? That is another matter entirely. And yet, fighting to the death as a last stand is a different matter to charging into the teeth of a superior enemy. One is a fight to extend your existence for as long as possible, the other actively seeks to end it sooner than is necessary.

A Space Marine of the Imperium, when faced with the choice, might decide to die in a manner of their own choosing. Magos Dallax is no Space Marine, however, and nor is she one of the skitarii, many of whom have little more free will than the kastelans, despite their biological parts. Dallax values her life enough to bite on the lure that Huron has left dangling.

'What alternative can you offer, traitor?'

The voice drips with all the scorn that can be mustered

through a vocal synthesiser, but even that cannot hide the desperate hope that lurks within. Magos Dallax may not agree to any alternative, but she will listen to it.

'A simple one,' Huron replies, as smoothly as he can despite his own vocal shortcomings. He was a great orator once – great enough to persuade the Lamenters and the Mantis Warriors to stand with his Chapter when he attempted to secede from the Imperium. His voice may have lost some of its charm, but the mind guiding it is, if anything, more finely developed. 'I propose that you and your charges walk out and join me.'

'Join you?' There is a harsh bark of binharic laughter. 'And become a traitor myself?'

'That is up to you,' Huron replies. 'You can choose to die today, of course – end your existence on this miserable rock, and fail in your duty to care for the automata under your command. Or you can preserve your life, secure their ongoing function, and survive. Should you choose to, you can die tomorrow, or the day after, or the day after that. I assure you that the galaxy is never short of ways to die, and my warband in particular is full of them. If you feel you have chosen poorly, all you need do is direct your kastelans to kill me, or one of my lieutenants. Then you can die a hero's death, striking at the Imperium's enemies. Perhaps you will even succeed. What I can assure you is that if you stay where you are, you will kill no more of my troops. I will simply leave you there, and call death down upon you in my own time.'

Footfalls of ceramite on metal reach Huron's ears. He did not bring many Space Marines with him, for this station did not require them, but the comm-bead in his ear tells him that they are all now on their way to his position. This is the last point of resistance in the complex, and they hunger for more combat.

They may not get it. He will have to see.

'You would take my machines from me!' Dallax accuses.

'Why should I?' Huron asks. 'If you join me, you will direct them as I command you. If you refuse, I will kill you then, instead of now.'

'You consort with hereteks and abominations!' Dallax asserts. 'They will seek to corrupt my charges!'

'Then kill them,' Huron says.

'Kill them?'

'Of course.' Huron chuckles. 'I prize loyalty to me. I am unconcerned about minor infighting. If some warpsmith or adept of the Dark Mechanicum attempts to take what is yours, kill them. If they have overreached themselves so greatly, and miscalculated their abilities so badly, I have little use for them in any case.'

Huron waits while Dallax considers this. The Adeptus Mechanicus, like most of the Imperium, is a place of strict hierarchies. Dallax will be used to obeying the orders of her superiors, going where she is sent and performing the tasks to which she is assigned, and having to petition for resources from those who might not understand her immediate needs. Huron knows that despite the fact the Machine Cult professes to despise such weak, human concepts as emotions, its adepts can become very attached to the machines for which they are responsible.

The notion of freedom enforced by strength, the freedom to adapt or innovate away from the Mechanicus' hidebound regulation, might hold appeal to a certain mind. As might a life where someone who threatens a machine, or denies the machine something it needs, can simply be killed with no repercussions.

These perceived freedoms are a lie, of course. But they are perhaps more honest lies than the ones peddled by the Imperium.

'I would not corrupt machine-spirits for you,' Dallax says, and Huron grins.

'I would not expect you to. I am interested in the results, not the methods. If you can achieve what I require without resorting to such techniques, I will not censure you.'

This is the true lure of Chaos. Not the sensual blandishments of the Dark Prince, or the mindless slaughter of the Lord of Skulls: for all that they are gods of Chaos, they have their own rules, and they bend their adherents to their will in their own way. No, this is the appeal of Chaos in the sense that it is the opposite of order, that it will upset convention, and bring about change. A Space Marine Chapter Master might declare himself planetary governor in order to better use the assets of his system; he might hoard resources to put them to best use, and when his supposed masters attempt to bring him to heel, he might turn on them and deny their right to command him and his warriors.

A Cybernetica datasmith might ponder the wisdom of a doctrine which declares that she should die fruitlessly in defence of a mining complex already lost to the enemy. She might consider that even if she should somehow survive, she will surely be executed and her robots redistributed, once her superiors discover her supposed failure.

Besides, there is no reason why saving herself, and her precious automata, need lead to corruption. Perhaps she can resist the temptation to stray from the Omnissiah's light. Perhaps she can even do good, by driving corruption out of other machines, with five kastelans to back her up. Perhaps she can pick a moment to deal some damage to the Red Corsairs from the inside, and actually aid the Imperium in a far more meaningful manner than a few drops more blood spilled in a mining complex already awash with it.

And as Huron has already pointed out, Dallax can always choose to die tomorrow.

The Space Marines of the Red Corsairs have arrived now, in blood-coloured armour adorned with the cracked emblems of their previous allegiances and scrawled over with new dedications. Some seek the patronage of one dark power or another, others honour all four, while still others claim no master at all save for themselves; and Huron Blackheart, of course.

Huron signals them, and they raise their weapons and ready themselves. If Dallax refuses, Huron will withdraw from the complex and level it. If Dallax claims to accept, she will walk through that doorway in the company of five deadly battle automata. A tech-priest who has been overcome by a desire to sell her life dearly might choose that method to get as close as she can to as many of the enemy as possible, before breaking her word and ordering her charges to attack. Huron is taking no chances: he is favoured by the warp, thanks to the bargains he made decades ago, but only a fool trusts that the power of Chaos will always, reliably, keep him safe.

The gods do love their little jokes.

'Very well,' Griza Dallax says, her augmented voice heavy with trepidation. 'I agree to your offer.'

'I agree to your offer, *lord*,' Huron corrects her. 'You need not mean the honorific, but I will have it from you.'

A pause.

'I agree to your offer, lord,' Dallax repeats, and if her voice is flat and emotionless, who can fault her? Not Huron. He knows that where the voice leads, the mind will often follow. When Dallax starts to repeat Huron's title without having to think about it, then a part of her brain will, on some level, have accepted it.

'We are done here,' Huron declares. 'We will commence

withdrawal. If you truly wish to accept my offer, magos, you will deactivate your robots' combat protocols and lead them out here.'

He waits. He is not impatient. The Imperium's fear of a machine-intellect means that any entirely cybernetic creation must have no will of its own. It can only be programmed by another, and that involves removing and replacing the sanctified doctrina wafers. The Mechanicus' battle automata are not best suited to quickly react to a rapidly changing combat situation, but once they have been given their orders, they are fearsomely effective at prosecuting them.

Finally, he hears the heavy tread of gigantic metal feet. The Red Corsairs move into deadly readiness, for although they are renegades and heretics they are still Adeptus Astartes, still the finest mortal warriors in the galaxy.

The first automata steps through the doorway. Huron stares up at it, waiting for the first twitch of its arms or canopy weapon mount which will suggest that it is about to attack; waiting for his Hamadrya to squeal an alarm, and the air to thicken around him as the gifts of the warp speed his senses and cloud the vision of his enemies to ward him from harm.

Nothing happens. The automata steps forward and is followed by another, and another. Then, shuffling along between them, comes the red-robed figure of Magos Griza Dallax.

She is tall enough to look Huron in the eye, but the frame beneath her robes is whip-thin instead of the massively bulky physique of a Space Marine, and the eyes that can be seen beneath the cowl of her hood are myriad and mechanical. She looks Huron up and down, taking in the blood-soaked magnificence of his power armour, and focusing on the dead flesh and cybernetic augmentations of his face and neck.

'Magos,' Huron says with a grin. 'So glad you could join

us. I'm sure you'll find your place without delay.' He raises his voice as far as he can, and the broken crackle of it snaps out harder than a power lash. 'Back to the *Spectre*! I want this station burning and us back into the warp within the hour!'

His Space Marines relax from their readiness and move smoothly from covering the automata with their boltguns to heading at pace for the landing craft in a clatter of ceramite footfalls. Huron turns away from his newest ally and points at the man in the Iron Guard uniform, who drops to one stained knee again.

'You. Take your team and check that area for anything valuable.' He smiles, and spittle dribbles from his dead lips. 'I advise you to hurry.'

'Yes, lord!' the man stammers, and he and his followers break into a run, weaving between the passive kastelans and heading for the doorway. Dallax flinches away from them, as though expecting an attack, but none comes. Huron ignores the tech-priest, and walks back through the bloodstained corridors.

Dallax will follow, or she will not. If she follows, she will live, at least for a while. If she stays, she will die.

It is no true choice, but it is the same choice the Imperium gives its citizens every day.

TWO

The *Spectre of Ruin* is a battle-barge, and it is the fist of a god rendered in plasteel, ferrocrete and adamantium. Seven and a half miles long, it bristles with weapons ranging from orbital bombardment cannons to fusion beamers. It is the equal of a fleet of lesser vessels. It is millennia old, and a monarch amongst void craft.

To Griza Dallax, it is as though she has been allowed entry to a most holy shrine, only to find it desecrated.

Griza has never been aboard a Space Marine vessel before, for she has never been assigned to any of the noble Chapters that make up humanity's defenders. What she has heard of such ships painted them as quiet, austere places, where the Adeptus Astartes warriors spend their time drilling, maintaining their weapons and wargear, and perhaps – depending on the Chapter and its traditions – engaging in contemplative meditation. There will be serfs wearing the Chapter uniform, proud to serve, utterly dedicated and trained to be fearsomely skilled in combat, although still no match for the transhuman warriors who are their masters. Techmarines, initiates into the mysteries of Mars, will work alongside tech-priests to repair vehicles, and maintain the ship itself. The entire vessel will be a place of order and calm purpose, except for when combat is joined, at which point it will become an icon of focused fury.

There is nothing ordered about the *Spectre of Ruin*. There is nothing calm about it, either. There is very little that is focused, although Griza acknowledges to herself that the 'fury' part is certainly present.

Entire corridors are filled with combat, as gangs of mortal warriors who did not get their fill of bloodletting in Station Delta-Kappa-39006 tear into each other. Some, through red-stained teeth, call for their deeds to be witnessed, and the names they beseech send shivers of disgust through Griza's body. She knows that those who have forsaken the Imperium worship false gods, but she has little understanding of such matters, since they do not concern circuits, gears or power transference. She never expected to hear syllables that seem to weigh heavier on the universe than the others that surround them. The sensation and her reaction to it bother her almost equally, for is it not a most irrational concept? And yet her perception, whilst potentially flawed, is undeniable.

She does not go into those corridors, and looks for a different route, but she finds little comfort elsewhere. The ancient symbols of the Astral Claws have not been removed, but ruined, and the constant reminder of the desecration of this vessel is an unpleasant shadow at the back of her mind, like the sensation of an intermittently glitching motor.

The *Spectre of Ruin* has changed in more profound ways, as well: in some places corrosion has crept across surfaces that should have been resistant to it, while in others, the internal structures appear to have melted and warped like heated wax. Here and there, Griza sees indentations and bulges in the walls which give the suggestion of screaming human faces trapped in the metal, and she is not convinced that it is decoration. The *Spectre* is not an unrecognisable, blighted hellscape, for enough of it remains unchanged for it to be clear what its form and purpose originally were, but if anything that makes it worse.

It is the difference between discovering the ashes where a body has been incinerated, and finding a person who has been horrendously burned, but who still lives to draw pain-wracked breath.

Griza does not go unchallenged during her wanderings. She travelled up to the battle-barge on a drop-ship along with Huron himself, and none of the warriors with him offered her harm, despite the glances cast in her direction. As soon as they reached the *Spectre of Ruin* she left the Blackheart behind, for there was no suggestion from him that she should not, but now she is in his realm and surrounded by those who know the Imperium only as an enemy. She has deactivated the combat protocols of her maniple, but has maintained those that command them to protect her from immediate harm. It is a good thing that she has done so.

Three men come at her first, with wide eyes and wider smiles, screaming challenges.

'Blood for the Blood God!'

They each carry twin chainblades, and their visible skin – of which there is a lot – is marked with the raised, discoloured lines of multiple scars. They see only a foe against which to test themselves.

Two of her maniple are equipped with power fists. Three

swings; three sizzling, wet impacts; three followers of Chaos flying through the air with flash-burned cavities where their torsos used to be. None of them got within five yards of her. Griza sees eyes watching her from shadows, and wonders if word will begin to carry about the *Spectre*'s newest arrivals, and if so, whether that will encourage others to leave her alone, or the boldest to seek her out to test her.

She has insufficient data to properly calculate probabilities, so she relegates the issue to background cogitation. She needs to find a place to charge her automata, especially since their continued operation will be key to her ongoing wellbeing, both for immediate protection and to ensure that she can, if called upon, at least potentially obey the orders of Huron Blackheart. However, she lacks the schemata for the *Spectre* to know where to begin in such a search, even assuming – given the alterations she has already witnessed – this vessel would still correspond to such a diagram. She wonders if there are any crew members who might be willing to assist her.

Wait.

Griza realises that she has not updated her logic files to reflect newly received information. She is still approaching matters as though she was on a Mechanicus ship, and she most assuredly is not. There is a more direct method to solve her current problem – one that would never work in the situations to which she is accustomed, but which is entirely appropriate in her current surroundings.

She sets off with new determination, marching in the midst of her dauntless bodyguard, and now she does not avoid others, but seeks them out. She happens upon a small group of crewers dressed in ragged clothes, with the lean physiques of those whom hard labour has shaped, and each one with a blade or gun in their belt. They eye her distrustfully, and her kastelans even more so, for they are as insects to the mighty battle automata.

'Who're you supposed to be?' one asks. He might be their nominal leader, or might simply be the most curious, or one who speaks first, or perhaps – given the powers to which this vessel is now dedicated – merely the only one left with an intact tongue. It is irrelevant.

'I am Cybernetica Datasmith Griza Dallax, and I require an arcflood outflow,' Griza announces. 'Which of you will assist me?'

The man sneers. 'Well, you can go–'

She shoots him.

She carries a gamma pistol. It is an ancient and powerful weapon, and one that by itself would be enough to give many enemies pause. The same could be said of her left arm, the end of which is enclosed in a powered gauntlet of similar potency to those wielded by her charges. Griza is far from incapable of defending herself, but her survivability is going to be greatly increased by her maniple being at full power.

The man collapses backwards, dead and burned before he hits the ground. Griza fights down her own biological reaction, as a stomach that for so long has subsisted on nothing but Mechanicus-approved nutrient bars twists, and threatens to betray her. She has never killed in cold blood before, but she is surrounded by enemies here, and strength is the only language many of them will understand. Not only that, but killing them practically counts as her duty. She just needs to not kill anyone too valuable to Huron Blackheart.

'I state again,' she says, and her voice synthesiser keeps the words level. 'I require an arcflood outflow. Which of you will assist me?'

The cowed crew members direct her to a small chamber.

Once, the outflow here would have been used to re-energise power packs for lascannons, and its output is sufficient for her purposes. She has to improvise the reagents required for the rites of energy transference, and offers a prayer to the Omnissiah as she does so. It will offer scant protection against the corrupted motive force likely to be offered by this vessel, but it is all she can do. Such a practice would be reason for grave censure amongst the priesthood, but she is beyond their reach here, and necessity forces her mechadendrites.

As she attaches the first two of her maniple to the outflow, sirens begin to wail. Griza knows that sound; it is the warning of an imminent translation to the warp. She realises that she has no idea, none whatsoever, how the ships of traitors and heretics move through the immaterium. Do they use Navigators? Do they even have Geller fields? They presumably must, for otherwise the mortal crew whom she encountered would surely not have survived their last voyage. She cannot believe that merely aligning oneself with such dark forces – as if *merely* is an appropriate term! – would be enough to guarantee safety from the unfettered danger of an unshielded warp jump.

The translation is hard, and it feels like her bionic and mechanical components are being shaken apart from each other by vibrations that exist nowhere apart from within herself, but it is over reasonably quickly, and there are no further complications. She remains alert for another ten minutes, but everything stays as it should, and she cannot hear anything from outside the chamber to suggest that the rest of the vessel's occupants have succumbed to translation sickness and are attempting to kill each other.

Well, no more than before, anyway.

Griza prepares to enter rest. Although her biological brain is boosted and augmented by cybernetic enhancements, she still requires actual sleep if she is to function at optimal levels. Something tells her that she will need all of her faculties if she is going to survive the challenges of her new existence.

She programs the other three kastelans to sentry mode, to immediately wake her with a warning signal if someone approaches, and to engage and destroy should that occur. She also sets a backup routine to wake her in any case after four hours, to change over the re-energising protocols and let two others take a turn.

Then, not without the echoes of what she recognises as trepidation, Griza Dallax turns her brain off.

THREE

The *Spectre of Ruin* has served as Huron's flagship since before the Imperium betrayed him, and he knows it as intimately as the weapons he carries. It has changed over time, of course, and no one who set foot on it now could mistake it for an Imperial vessel. The aquilas have been hacked off or broken, the great cat's head symbol of the Astral Claws has been painted over with the clenched black claw of the Red Corsairs, and the eight-pointed star of Chaos has been scratched here and there, in honour of the gods it now serves.

The personnel have altered as well, as would be expected. The neat-uniformed crewers of the ship's Imperial days are nowhere to be seen, but that does not mean that the *Spectre* is now lost to the mindless and the deranged. To be a bridge officer is to be under the eye of Huron Blackheart himself, and while that is a position in which failure is seldom tolerated, it holds authority, and some degree of security. Many of those who still operate the auspexes, vox, weapons control and so forth were the Chapter-serfs of the Astral Claws before their masters turned their backs on their old identities. These mortals' allegiances changed when their Chapter's did; those whose did not were quickly disposed of.

Despite all the changes – the carved skulls that leer down from spikes; the ritually scarred skin of the mortals, and the tusked helms of Huron's Terminator huscarls; the air itself holding the ever-present tang of human blood; the countless minor mutations; the fact that some of the crewers are now welded to their stations by the fusing of flesh and metal from the bleed-through of unholy warp energy – the bridge of the *Spectre of Ruin* is no free-for-all. Huron demands efficiency and obedience, and he gets it. For all the bargains he has made, the Blood Reaver has not lost himself, and he will not let his followers succumb, either.

Many mortals have sought to use the power of Chaos as a tool for their own ends, and most have been undone by their hubris. Huron Blackheart still balances on the razor's edge, not overly committed to any one of the Ruinous Powers, whilst still benefitting from their gifts. He would be a mighty prize for any of the gods to claim solely as their own, but he is too wily to be caught in any one snare – at least for now.

Still, he cannot allow himself to become overconfident.

'Lord?' a voice crackles over his personal vox. It's Hrafl Skarvjelsson, a former Space Wolf who had chafed at the ties of loyalty and duty that shackled him to the will of his Wolf Lord, and kept him from fighting as and where he chose.

'Speak,' Huron replies. Skarvjelsson is one of the warriors currently guarding the mighty blast doors that allow entry to the bridge. Huron suspects he knows what the issue is.

'There's a Mechanicus priest here with five battle robots. Is she one of ours?'

'At the moment,' Huron replies, smiling to himself. 'Does she wish to enter?'

'So she says.'

'Then let her do so.' Huron turns to face the doors.

Skarvjelsson does not question further. The mighty doors begin to grind aside, ponderously but smoothly, for Huron ensures that the systems on his flagship are properly maintained by his tech-adepts. Magos Dallax enters, surrounded as before by her kastelans.

The magos already carries herself differently, Huron notes. She was cautious and timid when she walked amongst his warriors on the return from Station Delta-Kappa-39006, as though expecting his offer to be a trap that would be sprung at any moment. Now she stands tall and strides with confidence, or at least is attempting to give that impression. She has already learned that deference is of little use in the Red Corsairs, save towards those who have the power to destroy her.

Her robots have changed as well. Huron gestures towards them with the bladed fingers of the Tyrant's Claw.

'Magos, I'm glad you've come. And I see you've redecorated.'

Dallax does not look at her charges. Their ceramite hides are now streaked with blood, which at least partially obscures the cog symbol of her faith.

'It has become clear to me that should I not wish to attract more attention than necessary, appearances had to be altered,' she declares, her tone stiff with guilt and defiance. 'Lord,' she adds, after a second. She is still fearful: partly that this is a convoluted and deadly joke at her expense, but also that she will have no real recourse should he indulge in the mockery she clearly believes may be coming.

Huron declines to do so. Even for a warlord with his resources, five battle automata and a knowledgeable datasmith to control them is nothing to sneer at. She is a new prize, and one which he will settle into place, given the chance. There is no point in putting her back up.

'Where did you get the blood?' he enquires mildly.

'My decision was taken in the aftermath of an attack which occurred on my way here,' Dallax says crisply. It is impossible to tell, given the inexpressive lenses which form her optical processors, but Huron gets the distinct impression that the magos is avoiding meeting his eyes. 'The fluids you see were no longer of use to those from whom they came, and serve the purpose of bringing our appearance more closely into line with the perceived average on this vessel.'

A very Mechanicus way of saying that she had her robots smear themselves in the blood of their dead enemies to make them look more like followers of the Ruinous Powers. Huron smiles, but does not push the matter further. It would not serve his purposes to do so.

'You felt our translation back out of the warp?' Huron asks her.

'I did,' Dallax agrees. 'It was why I came here. I wished to know where we are.' There is the faint hint of wonder in her voice. She has approached the master of this ship, killing those who opposed her, because she was curious about something. A far cry, Huron knows, from her previous existence.

And there, once more, is the lure of this life. The Imperium is a great stickler for rules and procedures, but like most such things, they are in place to benefit those who created them. Dallax could have theoretically turned her kastelans on a superior whose dogmatic adherence to regulations frustrated her intentions, but it would have been her doom. Here, as someone who is not herself weak, and who commands an unquestioningly obedient force of concentrated strength,

Magos Dallax is coming to terms with the fact that she has a lot more freedom to do as she pleases.

Huron has seen this before, and always takes pleasure in watching the cauls drop from the eyes of others.

'Welcome to my home, magos,' Huron says, extending the Tyrant's Claw towards the enormous, curving viewport that forms the front of the *Spectre of Ruin*, now the shutters to shield the crew from the mind-twisting realities of the warp have been retracted. 'Or one of them, at any rate. But I like this the best. This is New Badab.'

The *Spectre* is pitching forwards very slightly as he speaks, and he hears a faint buzz that could well be the equivalent of a gasp of awe or shock emanate from Dallax's vocal unit. In front of them, the orb of a world comes into view.

It is in no way a recreation of Badab Primaris, the home world of the former Astral Claws, and from where Huron ruled the sector in the manner of one of the great warrior-kings of old. It is simply a world that Huron has found and taken as his own. He had less than three hundred renegade Space Marines with him when he stumbled across it as the remains of his fleet fled from the Imperium's hounds, but even that number of gene-smithed warriors were sufficient to subdue the warring, ragtag bands of mutants and twisted humans that had populated it. Many of the survivors flocked to Huron's banner, recognising his strength, while the remainder cower in the areas in which he has no interest, and live out their short and brutish lives killing each other over meagre resources, personal insults and what passes for theological disagreements.

'We are... in the Maelstrom?' Dallax asks.

'We are indeed,' Huron replies. 'When I first came here, it was the second-largest spatial vortex in the galaxy, second only to the Eye of Terror. Now, of course, Abaddon has ripped realspace apart and subsumed the Maelstrom into his Great Rift, but I still know where the borders lie. I can feel them in my bones.'

He notices that Dallax stiffens at his mention of the Warmaster's name, and stifles a phlegmy chuckle. What would she think if she knew that he had stood in front of Abaddon the Despoiler and parlayed with him, one warlord to another? Huron acknowledged Abaddon's strength, of course, and paid lip service to him as the greatest warlord of the Ruinous Powers, but he is no Black Legion toady. The Red Corsairs are their own power, and they answer the Warmaster's call to arms as and when they see fit.

Huron will join the Black Crusade, of course, but he is doing so in his own time, and in his own way. The raid on the Mechanicus mining complex was a trivial diversion while he waits for elements of his force to assemble.

'How is it that I can see solid ground?' Dallax asks. 'The warp is energy, I know this to be true. What is this planet?'

Tagron, one of Huron's huscarls, snorts in amusement behind the tusked helm of his Tactical Dreadnought armour. He is no turncoat from another Chapter, but a former Astral Claw who fought in the Badab War. The ignorance of the Imperium amuses him now, just as it does Huron, for all the fact that a century ago, they themselves knew little more of such matters.

'The warp overlaps with the material world here,' Huron tells the confused tech-priest. 'It is neither one thing, nor the other. Can you not see the immaterium bleeding through even now?'

He gestures past New Badab, for the planet does not hang in front of the cold blackness of space, filled with the pinpricks of distant stars. Instead it is backed by faint, dark whorls of unnatural colour, as though the heavens themselves have been bruised. The shapes and swirls within it do not move while you look directly at them, but in the corner of your eye they appear to coil, slow and languorous, like lazily mating serpents. This is not the true face of the warp, which can send mortals mad in seconds, and which few other than Navigators can even bear, let alone make sense of, but it contains echoes of that power. To live under these skies for a prolonged period of time is a recipe for damnation, and the erosion of one's sanity.

'And this is your home?' Dallax asks, her voice thin with horror.

'One of them,' Huron says. 'Down there is the Palace of Thorns, and the greatest stronghold of my power. Hundreds of thousands of warriors – human, xenos, mutant and Adeptus Astartes. Thousands of war machines, weapons beyond count. And do you see the fleet?'

'I see them, lord,' Dallax replies.

The clusters of running lights are not easy to pick out against the planet or the unnatural sky beyond it, at least not at first, but Huron watches as Dallax's lenses click and whirr faintly while she focuses and refocuses. There are perhaps a couple of hundred craft in orbit around New Badab at the moment, at the least, and that is not the full extent of the armada at his command: there are also the ships at Hell's Iris, and the smaller outposts at the Great Lesion and Helix Beta.

'It is an impressive force,' the magos says neutrally, and something nudges at Huron.

'Impressive?' he repeats. '*Impressive*, datasmith? I fled from the Imperium while half-dead, and at the head of the tattered remnants of my Chapter. In the decades since then I have forged a fighting force capable of breaking a segmentum, should I wish to break it!' He snorts. 'Abaddon's might is greater, but I have had less than a century to build my power, and Abaddon has had a hundred times that. The First Legions bleat of their history, and mock us as thin-blooded newcomers to their so-called Long War, but where are their primarchs, whose legacy they cling to so tightly? Horus and Curze are dead, and Alpharius' name is bandied about by uncountable rudderless warbands. The Ultramarines claim to have killed him on Eskrador, but I saw the reports from the Danevra Subsector. Still, if those wretches of the Alpha Legion know anything, they're not sharing. And what of the rest? Angron, Perturabo, Fulgrim and Lorgar hide themselves in the depths of the Eye, being precisely no use to anyone, and it took ten thousand years for Mortarion and Magnus to stir themselves. They...'

He pauses as Dallax makes a choking noise, then dead lips peel apart in a grin that reveals his pointed teeth. The Hamadrya chitters as it tastes her fear, and approves.

'You did not know?' he asks softly. 'You thought the Death Lord and the Crimson King were still mere tales that would never trouble your precious Imperium again?'

'Those names,' Dallax says weakly. Huron can see that the power of them has struck her, but she does not understand why. 'Who...?'

Huron barks a laugh. 'I still forget how much the Imperium likes to cover up its own mistakes. Pray you never find the answer to your question, magos.' He sighs. 'I'll say this for Abaddon, he's stirred the galaxy up properly this time. The daemon primarchs have come forth with all the pomp and self-importance you would expect from them, and things will never be the same again.'

'Is it inevitable?' Dallax whispers, her voice merely the ghost of static. 'Is the Imperium truly doomed?'

Huron's smile diminishes slightly. He wants to see the Imperium torn apart as much as anyone. He wants it to feel the agony he felt after the meltagun blast from that bastard

Androcles vaporised half his body and nearly killed him. He wants its lies and empty promises of protection exposed, and for its mewling populace to scream their damnation of the Emperor before they die, as they too taste His betrayal.

He wants all these things, and while he would have liked to be the architect of them, he will not begrudge its occurrence simply because Abaddon the Despoiler brings them about instead. However, Huron Blackheart was always wily, and the warp is now his close companion. His cabals of sorcerers do his bidding, and scry for guidance, but he also has his own dark dreams, and they do not scream of the Warmaster's assured victory. After all, it was not Abaddon's entreaties that dragged Mortarion and Magnus forth from their sulking.

It was the knowledge that their brother had woken.

Roboute Guilliman is revitalised and on the move, as Huron knows very well. A century ago, Huron might have been awestruck at the notion of potentially meeting the Master of Macragge, let alone fighting alongside him. Any such desire would have turned to ash even before the culmination of the Badab War, however, for although the Imperium was happy to let the Ultramarines rule over the Five Hundred Worlds, they could not countenance the Astral Claws being in command of even a single sector. Guilliman's legacy is just another example of the Imperium's hypocrisy.

That does not mean that the primarch of the Ultramarines himself is to be underestimated. Huron cannot see the future, and has little patience for anyone who claims they can with any reliability, but despite the fact that Abaddon has riven the galaxy in two, the Blood Reaver cannot see a clear path to the Warmaster's final victory. It might occur, or it might not. Huron himself already has agents in play, but he will not commit fully to Abaddon's scheme until he knows–

He looks up sharply, as senses beyond those enjoyed by most mortals alert him to something. The Hamadrya gibbers on his shoulder.

'Warp wake!' the Master of Auspex barks. 'Lord, I'm reading a significant incoming warp wake, *very* significant!'

Huron is already moving towards his command station. 'Give me an estimate of size,' he orders. He knows it is a difficult request to answer, but he is not as capricious a master as many who follow the Ruinous Powers. Those that serve him well have little to fear from him, and so rather than cowering from his perceived displeasure, they give their utmost.

'Perhaps... thirty capital ships,' the auspex officer says tightly, 'translating in close formation.'

'Weapons ready, shields at full power!' Huron roars, and his vocal implants take over to ease the strain on his damaged voice. 'Broadcast a general alert to the rest of the fleet, and get the boarding crews to their assault craft!'

His ships will far outnumber these incoming vessels, but they are spread out in orbit all around New Badab. If this is an Imperial strike force, coming in fast and disciplined, they could cut his armada to ribbons if he can only engage them piecemeal. The *Spectre of Ruin* will be a strong bastion against such an attack, but even that will depend on the number and nature of the attackers. Although it is rare and powerful, the *Spectre* is far from alone in the galaxy: most Space Marine Chapters will have two or three battle-barges equivalent to Huron's flagship, and while it would be reckless, perhaps even foolhardy, to commit such ancient and valuable vessels to an attack this deep in the Maelstrom, that is not to say it cannot happen.

Huron clears his mind and assesses the situation, splitting his attention between the tactical read-outs that are popping up as hololiths, and the vista he can see with his own eyes.

The murmurings of the warp inside his mind, the voiceless warnings he experiences when danger is close, are silent; that does not mean he will assume that all is well. It is all too like the Ruinous Powers to extend their favour, and then withdraw it at a time that suits them best.

'Contacts!' the Master of Auspex calls, and shouts coordinates and trajectories. The gunnery officers start their calculations, traversing the *Spectre of Ruin*'s guns to draw a bead on the new arrivals into New Badab's territory. A battle-barge is not a vessel best equipped for ship-to-ship warfare – its primary purpose is to bombard a planet prior to launching an assault wave of Space Marines – but that is not to say it cannot hold its own, especially at shorter ranges. Should the intruders get close enough, of course, they will find out what it is like to be on the receiving end of Space Marine boarding parties; the trouble is that Huron only took a small complement of his finest on their raid, and so he cannot inflict the carnage that he would be able to under optimal conditions.

He looks at the tactical auspex as it begins to update with the information flooding into the *Spectre*'s sensors, and a chill runs through him.

'Warp's blood…' he breathes, acidic spittle trickling over his lower lip. 'What is that?'

'It's a, a–' the Master of Auspex stammers.

'Give me an ident!' Huron roars, his vocal synthesiser crackling with rage. He can see what it is, and he can see what accompanies it, but the name will tell him what he truly faces here.

The Master of Auspex turns to him with a face stricken of all emotion save despair. 'Lord, it's the *Macragge's Honour*, with twenty other vessels of significant size.'

A Gloriana-class battleship. Sixteen miles of crenellated

majesty, constructed in the days prior even to the Great Crusade, and bedecked with sufficient weaponry to annihilate a fleet of lesser vessels all by itself. It is a relic of a different time, from when humanity was full of vigour, and conquest of the galaxy looked to be nothing more than its destiny.

It is the flagship of Roboute Guilliman.

'Come about!' Huron orders, but even as his mind balks from the concept of going head-to-head with the *Macragge's Honour*, a small part of him thrills at the notion of facing a primarch on the field of battle. Guilliman's tactical genius was always viewed to be second to none, but that was ten thousand years ago. He woke back up into a galaxy that must have surely changed beyond recognition, and he has walked into the seat of Huron's power. Even primarchs can be overconfident.

Besides, two things remain true. The first is that although the identity of the Chapter that served as primogenitor of the Astral Claws' gene-seed has been lost in the Imperium's flawed and labyrinthine records system, the Ultramarines are reckoned to be a prominent candidate. It would amuse Huron greatly to go up against the primarch whose genetic material might well have created the body he now possesses.

The second is that he has clawed and spat and fought and dealt with powers almost beyond comprehension to keep that same body tethered to his spirit, and if his existence has to end, then attempting to deal a death blow to the Avenging Son seems like a worthwhile way to go.

He sucks in a breath.

'Prepare to–'

'We're being hailed by the *Macragge's Honour*!' the Mistress of Vox calls, and then cowers in anticipation of painful or fatal retribution, for she began to speak just as Huron did, and so spoke over him.

'Bring it up,' Huron orders. This is more important than disciplining a crew member.

Static hisses, and resolves into a voice. It is deep and powerful in a way that Huron's will never be again, but it is not the voice of a primarch. It is the voice of a Space Marine, and it is a voice that Huron recognises.

'Hail, Lord of the Maelstrom,' it booms. *'I return with spoils of war.'*

Huron's lips twist. He does not look at Dallax; he noted her sudden, desperate hope as the name of the new ship was announced, and he can sense her crushing despair as the reality is made clear to them all. The datasmith's emotional whiplash would have amused him at any other time, but this development is one to which he must give his full attention.

'Verngar,' he rasps in return. 'You haven't lost your flair for the dramatic, I see.'

FOUR

Lord Verngar the Apostate is, Huron supposes, every inch the image of a renegade Astartes. He is tall and hale, and his face is not yet so ruined by mutation or battle damage that he has lost his noble countenance, albeit a somewhat severe one. His armour was blood red already, for he was once an Angel Encarmine, one of the myriad sons of Sanguinius, but he was exiled from the Chapter for insisting that the Red Thirst that plagued them was in fact the touch of Chaos. Now the bat-winged blood drop on his pauldron has been replaced by the clenched claw of the Red Corsairs, and his armour is hung with grisly trophies.

None of this, however, is what troubles Huron. What troubles him is that Verngar is no mere Space Marine, renegade or otherwise; he is still a gifted commander and leader, and although he indulges the thirst for blood that comes upon him in combat, he does not collapse into the Black Rage and lose all reason. Verngar is supremely vicious, but he is still in control. Perhaps this is the result of some bargain of his own that he has struck with the gods of Chaos: Huron knows that this is well within the bounds of possibility. All in all, Verngar has the potential to rise even further within the ranks of the Red Corsairs than he already has, and that is in no way as peaceful a prospect as it would be in a loyalist Chapter.

Huron's Hamadrya chatters softly on his shoulder in warning, but he is already well aware of the dangers. None of the former Astral Claws have yet dared challenge his leadership, and he does not believe they would do so, but the newcomers? Those who have come to his side in the decades since the Badab War, enacting their own imitations of his grander betrayal of the Imperium in order to do so? They have less reason for loyalty, and now some of them are beginning to gain considerable power and influence through trickery, machinations and simple bloodletting.

He is in a nest of vipers, and he must watch his step.

'Lord?' Armenneus Valthex asks, and Huron realises the Master of the Forge is looking at him expectantly. As, indeed, is everyone else present.

Well, this is the war room of the Palace of Thorns. It is only to be expected.

Huron directs his glance briefly to Valthex, then back again to Verngar, who is standing on the opposite side of the hololith table with his helmet under his arm, and his mighty thunder hammer, Stormfiend, mag-clamped to his back. The Apostate somehow manages to convey both respectful attention and smug disregard with the same stance, so much so that he cannot reasonably be called on the latter without the speaker appearing paranoid or oversensitive, neither of which are good impressions to give in the Maelstrom. Huron waits for a few more seconds, simply to make it look like his pause was to deliberately study his underling rather than being momentarily lost in his own thoughts, then he speaks.

'You captured Roboute Guilliman?'

His voice crackles out through the room, a hiss of spite and machine static. Verngar bows his head, and replies in the rich tones of an uninjured Space Marine.

'Indeed, lord. Having been pulled into the Maelstrom by the machinations of Lord Magnus, Guilliman's fleet fell prey to our trap, as foreseen by Kairos Fateweaver.'

The left side of Huron's top lip curls into a slight sneer. He has little patience with daemons, even those of great renown. They are paltry reflections of their patrons, and Huron has never been of a temperament that easily tolerates dealing with lackeys. Daemons can be useful tools, but for all their power and supposed knowledge, they can still be tricked and outwitted by mortals. That makes them questionable allies at best, even assuming their intentions are genuine, which they almost certainly are not.

'It appears that congratulations are in order, Verngar,' he says, lacing his words with razors of acid politeness. 'And where is the primarch of the Ultramarines now? You have him with you? Bound somewhere in his own flagship, perhaps? That would be a delicious irony.'

Huron knows this is not the case. For one thing, Verngar is not the type to downplay his own achievements. If he had Guilliman with him then he would have announced it the moment he arrived, would have paraded the Lord of Ultramar in chains through the city surrounding the Palace of Thorns, and brought him into the war room to bask in the glory of his achievements.

More tellingly, Huron has already heard of how the fightback against Abaddon's predations is being coordinated by the resurrected primarch of the Ultramarines. Not even the Imperium's propaganda machine would dare to make such a claim if it did not have basis in reality.

The skin tightens slightly at the corners of Verngar's eyes. The peril of having an unruined face is that no movement is without a meaning that can be read by those with eyes to see it, let alone a warp creature on their shoulders which, rumour has it, allows Huron to hear the thoughts of those around him.

Huron cannot, in fact, do so, and has never claimed as such, although he has not quashed the rumours, either. However, he has always been both perceptive and intuitive, and since striking the bargain of which the Hamadrya was part, these abilities have been increased to a level that the Blood Reaver believes is likely beyond anything natural. He can detect falsehoods with ease, but a statement can be true and yet still mask the intention behind it, and the misled or uninformed can speak words they erroneously believe true with what appears to be total honesty. Nothing in life comes easily.

'I do not have Guilliman, lord,' Verngar replies solemnly. 'However, I do have–'

'How did he escape you?' Huron interrupts him. His other officers around the table – Valthex, Oneius Prayd, Katar Garrix, Garlon Souleater, and Warpsmith Turazan – are glancing back and forth between the two of them as they speak. Huron knows they will be searching for weakness, either for their own advancement or to ensure they do not tether themselves to a losing prospect. He intends to keep Verngar on the back foot.

'We imprisoned him in the Blackstone Fortress gifted to us by Lord Abaddon,' Verngar says, meeting Huron's eyes. There is the hint of defiance in his gaze, and Huron pauses for a moment. The Apostate still feels he has the advantage.

'And was this on the Fateweaver's orders?' Huron asks. It is a simple trap, but an effective one. To answer in the positive suggests that Verngar has given up his authority to a daemon; to deny it means that whatever has happened – and surely something must have happened, or Verngar would be far less guarded – is the Apostate's responsibility.

'Lord Kairos did indeed request that Guilliman be held by us,' Verngar replies. 'I saw no reason to disagree – after all, can there be many items of greater value in this galaxy than a primarch? Let alone the only surviving loyalist primarch. And besides, the place in which we held him had been given to Lord Huron by the Warmaster, and so surely it must be secure?'

Huron recognises that rhetorical tone, and sees no reason to play along with Verngar's intended direction. 'You have not yet explained how Guilliman escaped, Apostate.'

Verngar bows his head again, but his eyes do not leave Huron's. His deference is a sham, and his delays are calculated to set the scene in a manner that will favour him. 'Forgive me, Lord Huron. I was merely providing background to my explanation.'

'Get on with it, Apostate!' snaps Katar Garrix. Garrix is Huron's headsman, a skull-helmed warrior with an axe that stands taller than most mortals. He is a competent tactician at best, but few are more fearsome in battle. Many are the enemy champions who have fallen to his blade, and not a few Red Corsairs who have disappointed their lord beyond redemption, yet had the weakness to beg for their lives instead of attempting to kill Huron, and dying in combat with some nobility left to them.

However, Garrix is no fool. Huron knows that should his own position be seen as weak, there are few indeed who will stand by him out of loyalty. Valthex and Corpsemaster

Garreon, perhaps, probably because they are too closely associated with him for any new master of the Red Corsairs to be comfortable with their continued existence, but the motive is of less importance to Huron than the practicality. Garrix, however, is a butcher: a supremely talented one, but a butcher nonetheless. He lives to cause death, preferably in glorious single combat, but in the faceless brawl of a melee if necessary. He is not a creature to whom loyalty will come easily, provided any new master will still give him the opportunity to wet his axe in others' blood. For him to be so hostile to Verngar is a good sign.

'The escape occurred due to an unfortunate confluence of events,' Verngar replies, and while the glance he casts at Garrix is not overtly dismissive, it is flavoured with disdain.

'"Unfortunate" is a mild term for such a failure,' Huron bites out. 'Did you not just point out what a valuable asset Guilliman would be?'

'In this matter, my lord, the term is accurate,' Verngar retorts. 'Kairos Fateweaver's foresight somehow failed to discern the arrival of a mighty daemonic host of the Blood God, led by Skarbrand the Exiled One, who fell upon the fortress with the intention of taking Guilliman's head.'

'That seems like something the Fateweaver really should have predicted,' Oneius Prayd remarks dryly. Prayd is a former Red Scorpions captain, and fought against Huron during the Badab War, until his peers chose Carab Culin to lead the Chapter following the death of Verant Ortys. His festering resentment caused him to strike out with most of his company and lay waste to a string of xenos worlds before eventually finding their way to Huron's side, drawn by rumours that the Blood Reaver rewards his warriors on the merits of their achievements.

Verngar spreads his hands. 'If it was a ruse, then it was well played indeed, for the fighting between the forces of the two gods was vicious. We defended our positions, but were betrayed from within.' The Apostate looks at Huron, and now there is a challenge in his eyes. 'Were you aware, Lord Huron, that the Blackstone Fortress contained a gateway at the centre?'

Huron's teeth clench in reflexive anger. 'What manner of gateway?'

'One which allowed our enemies to enter without our knowledge,' Verngar says softly. 'An aeldari relic, I believe. The first we knew of it was when some of those xenos scum, and warriors who resembled Dark Angels, had already freed Guilliman and his host, and were attempting to depart the same way they had entered.' Verngar smiles thinly. 'It is hard indeed to defend a position when you have been left unaware of a hole in those same defences.'

He waits, and now Huron sees the trap that has been laid for him in turn. To claim knowledge of this gateway would suggest he deliberately left Verngar uninformed of such an important matter, which would be a grave oversight at best, and at worst would look like the sort of deliberate betrayal of an underling that might make others decide they would be safer with someone else controlling New Badab. To deny knowledge of it, which is the truth, suggests he does not know the nature of his own resources.

Thankfully, there is someone else who can take at least partial blame.

'I wondered what manner of surprise Abaddon's gift had for us,' Huron says, twisting his lips into a knowing smile. 'Tell me, Verngar, did you truly think the Warmaster would just *give* us a Blackstone Fortress? Does Abaddon the Despoiler strike you as a being afflicted with great generosity? I knew there had to be a catch in it somewhere. It appears you have discovered it for me, although I would have preferred a less costly price than letting the Master of Ultramar escape.'

Verngar's expression is guarded. This is not a full-throated power grab: not yet, at any rate. This is the prelude, the verbal fencing while they prepare their ground and before they even acknowledge their intentions, let alone make the first real lunge.

'Your point is well made, lord,' Verngar says, and he withdraws into himself a little. 'Despite that failure, I return to you bearing a gift worthy of the Lord of the Red Corsairs. The *Macragge's Honour*. It is a mighty vessel, and one that will serve you well.'

A well-played counter, Huron acknowledges silently. Even he cannot strike his commanders down without good reason – or at least a reason that his other commanders would accept as such – because an unpredictable and vindictive lord is a danger, and one who will garner more enmity than support. What manner of lord would call for Garrix's axe in response to being presented with a prize the magnitude of the *Macragge's Honour*?

An insecure one. And Huron has no intention of presenting himself as insecure.

However, there is a limit to how far he will go in the interests of how he is perceived by the others around the table. He is still Huron Blackheart, and he plays others rather than lets them play him. He refused to be cowed by the assembled might of the Imperium; he will not let it happen through clever words and fine gifts. Besides, Verngar has the gall to make a present of what should be Huron's by right. *Huron* bestows gifts, as and when he sees fit: his underlings offer him *tribute*.

'Keep it,' he says quietly.

Verngar's brows furrow, very slightly. Perhaps he anticipated buying his way back into favour, if his attempt to entrap and destabilise Huron failed. 'Lord Huron. You are refusing my gift?'

'I am,' Huron replies bluntly. 'The *Macragge's Honour* is a mighty warship, there is no doubt of that. It has also served the Ultramarines for ten thousand years, and the stink of their righteousness will be ground into its very metal. I am assuming Guilliman did not leave its crew behind – if he did, they will not serve you, and if he did not, the ship will not obey you. The machine-spirit itself will turn against you.'

'The wretches left on board are spineless, and the ship brought us here easily enough,' Verngar says, and now he sounds defensive for the first time.

'Aye, I expect it did!' Huron retorts. 'And had you commanded it to open fire on the *Spectre of Ruin,* I imagine it would have obliged you! Had you attempted to target an Imperial craft, I rather believe the targeting auspexes would be less than useless.' He tuts. 'It is a mighty prize, and perhaps would make fine bait, but it will be a long time indeed before I would trust that ship to fight for us.'

Huron notes that Valthex is nodding, for the Master of the Forge agrees with his assessment. Warpsmith Turazan, on the other hand, looks thoughtful. Perhaps he is considering matching his scrapcode against the machine-spirit of the *Macragge's Honour,* which is not a contest on which Huron would care to place a wager. Turazan is a master of fusing sorcery and machine, and there are few better at corrupting the technology of the Imperium, but a Gloriana-class battleship of this age and provenance is a different matter entirely. The fact that Guilliman himself used it as his flagship throughout the Great Crusade and the Horus Heresy is no mere item of trivia: the *Macragge's Honour* will not readily recognise the authority of anyone who is not a servant of its lord. It must be broken, and the breaking of it could be a lifetime's work.

'Then I thank you for this great gift, lord,' Verngar says with a bow, and it occurs to Huron that perhaps he has been outplayed after all. Now Verngar gets to keep his spoils, and while the ship may not serve him well immediately, all things can be corrupted with time. If Turazan gets involved to speed matters, Verngar might be able to consolidate a greater amount of power and influence amongst his peers and their followers. The Red Corsairs are held together by a web of influence, authority and loyalty just like their Imperial counterparts; however, unlike the loyalists, those strands can move and shift, rather than remaining tied to ranks.

There are few Imperial Chapters where the Chapter Master could be challenged for his position, since it is usually only vacated in death. In fairness, Huron knows that his position will only be vacated in death as well, but while that death might come at the hands of an Imperial assassin or a loyalist bolter shell, it could also come in the form of one of his own.

'Verngar,' he rasps, and the Apostate rises from his bow.

'Yes, lord?'

'Where have you been since Guilliman slipped your clutches?'

Verngar's gaze doesn't waver. 'We were occupied with defending the Blackstone Fortress, and ourselves, for some time. Skarbrand and Fateweaver fell on each other again after Guilliman's escape, and we were caught in the midst of that combat. After that we sought to make our way here, but' – he spreads his hands – 'it appears that on occasion the warp can be as fickle for the servants of the True Gods as it is for those that still worship the Emperor.'

Huron eyes him. Verngar did not return with a ragtag, battle-scarred mob, but at the head of a well-supplied war fleet. He has been building his power back up in the aftermath of his failure, which is by no means an unreasonable thing to do, for returning to New Badab while looking weak would be an invitation for another ambitious Corsair to seek to supplant him.

'Just remember,' Huron tells him. 'If I decide I do want that ship, I will take it from you.'

Verngar's expression does not change, but he nods slightly. 'Understood, lord. Of course.'

Huron holds his gaze for a few more seconds, then breaks it to look down and press the rune that activates the hololith table. It blinks into life and vomits a cloud of points of light into the air above it: a galactic map. The great green tear of the Cicatrix Maledictum rips its way almost from edge to edge, thicker here and thinner there, but still dividing the galaxy in two. Although it originated from the Eye of Terror, the greatest blot of the giant rift is around the Maelstrom, being far closer to the galactic centre.

'Here, then, is the Warmaster's handiwork,' Huron declares, sweeping the Tyrant's Claw through the hololith and letting the light play over the blackened, pitted metal of its fingers. 'We delayed Guilliman, but he slipped through our fingers, and you may be certain that Abaddon will hear of that. So the question for us now is, how can we best turn this situation to our advantage? Do we rally to the Despoiler's banner and join with him as he beats upon the walls of Terra once more?'

'Do we know that to be his goal?' Valthex asks.

'Please, Forgemaster,' Turazan says with a snort. 'Abaddon is nothing if not predictable. He holds ten thousand years of bitterness for his primogenitor's death – where else will he be going?'

'Do not speak of the Warmaster in such a manner,' Garlon Souleater puts in, his voice as resonant as a bell. Of all of them, he is the only one who has not removed his helm. It has been many years since he has last done so, and Huron is no longer certain that he can. Not that it matters.

'Lord Huron has no fear of Abaddon,' Turazan retorts. 'Why should I?'

'Because you are not Lord Huron,' Garlon says simply, and the matter-of-fact tone of his voice removes any further replies from the warpsmith's lips.

Huron glares at them for the interruption. He does not fear Abaddon, that much is true, although he wonders whether that is simply because the capacity for such an emotion was removed from him at the same time as he underwent all the other arcane processes that raised him into the transhuman brotherhood of the Astartes. He is wary of the Warmaster though, and who wouldn't be? Abaddon has made his own bargains with the Ruinous Powers, and ones deeper and deadlier than Huron's, he has no doubt of that.

'So do we assist the Warmaster, and risk his wrath for being unable to present him with his foe bound and helpless?' Huron asks, with a glance at Verngar. 'Or do we make our own move, seek to profit from these events in some other manner, and risk the Warmaster's vengeance at a later date should he decide to take issue not only with our failure, but also our unwillingness to answer his call?'

There is silence while the Red Corsairs commanders study the hololith. Then Huron sees a smile creep over the face of Verngar.

'I believe,' the Apostate says, 'I may know a way to do both.'

FIVE

'That is a bold statement, Verngar,' Armenneus Valthex says. 'Especially since you have only just returned from your misfortune at the Blackstone Fortress.'

Armenneus Valthex, Master of the Forge and the Alchemancer, watches Verngar carefully. The Apostate is a relative newcomer: within the most recent twenty-three point two per cent of Space Marines who have joined the Red Corsairs, according to the data. His rise has been notable, and his ambition obvious. That is unsurprising, since although a sizeable portion of the Astartes warriors under Huron's command seek nothing except battle – now free of the constraints placed upon them by the Imperium, in contravention of the very purpose for which they were created – most of the rest desire power. Few have much concept of loyalty beyond that which is convenient.

Valthex, however, has not shed those trappings of his former life as an Astral Claw. Huron Blackheart is no longer his Chapter Master, but he is still his lord, and Valthex will serve and protect him. Part of his loyalty is down to the sunk costs that Huron represents, for Valthex has invested a lot of time and effort into the preservation of his master, including making his own bargains where necessary. Part of it is because his devotion to Huron is well known, and so any warrior seeking to depose the Blood Reaver will surely seek to remove Valthex immediately afterwards, if not before. In that sense, protecting Huron is self-preservation.

However, more than that, Valthex still believes in Huron. He was right to defy the Imperium's ridiculous edicts, he was right to resist when it attempted to reimpose its will, and he was right to flee rather than die pointlessly. The Imperium needs to have its own flaws and failings laid out for it to see, and Valthex knows of no one better to do that than Huron Blackheart.

'It is through my experiences there that I am able to make such a claim,' Verngar says with a hint of haughtiness. 'We all know that Abaddon has been able to activate the Blackstone Fortresses and access their power and weapons systems, such as in the Gothic War, but his methods are still a mystery. Rumours vary, from bargains with the gods themselves, to the ritual use of objects imbued with their own power. I presume Lord Huron gained no insight from the Despoiler when he was presented with our fortress?'

'The fortress itself was enough,' Huron growls. 'I had no reason to tie us more tightly to him by begging for the methods to activate it. Such is the way of the Ruinous Powers and those in thrall to them – they will offer a gift, but leave you wanting more, something they will claim that only they are able to provide. So you pay their price, and get the power, but that also has flaws, and once again, only they can offer the solution. And so it continues, until your soul is lost and your will is enslaved, and you are nothing but a puppet with your power entirely beholden to another's whims.' The Blood Reaver coughs out something that might have been a laugh. 'I know these snares, Verngar, and I will not step into them, especially not when they are set by a warrior who feels threatened by the rise of the Red Corsairs.'

Valthex smiles in response to his lord's words, which are strong and bold. However, doubt lurks in his chest like a waiting predator. He and Garreon combined their knowledge to produce the biomechanical miracle that has maintained Huron's body since the retreat from the Palace of Thorns, but it was not this that brought his spirit back. That was something else, a manifestation of which is the Hamadrya that accompanies the Master of the Maelstrom. Huron made bargains while his soul drifted on the tides of the warp, and no one knows exactly with whom or what those bargains were made, or what coin the Blood Reaver used.

What Valthex *does* know is that the gene-seed of the Astral Claws is degrading. Garreon is at Hell's Iris even now, working on their remaining stock prior to implanting it in those prospects who survive the punishing selection process, but the Corpsemaster has voiced his concerns to Valthex before. Neither of them have ever heard of an attrition rate so rapid, and the amount of obvious mutations within the ranks of those former Astral Claws who still live is growing. Huron has seized gene-seed from other Chapters, and new Red Corsairs are still being forged, but the core of their genetic heritage to the Astral Claws is being winnowed away.

Perhaps that is no bad thing: the Astral Claws were created by the Imperium, and divided from their brothers by the

Imperium's artificial limitations on numbers and organisation. The Red Corsairs are united in mindset and purpose, not biology. Nonetheless, Valthex finds himself wondering about what it was that Huron traded in exchange for his return, and the occult protection he now enjoys.

'Then since I have failed you by allowing Guilliman to escape, and I cannot offer you tribute with the *Macragge's Honour*, allow me to serve in another way,' Verngar says to Huron. 'While I was with Kairos Fateweaver in the Blackstone Fortress, the daemon made mention of an artefact that might be capable of activating it – the Ebon Talon.'

'Have we not already established that the Fateweaver's words cannot be trusted, and his perceptions may not even be accurate?' Oneius Prayd retorts. 'This is as likely to be a trap, a mistake or a game as it is to be reliable information. Daemons always seek to deceive.'

Valthex smiles to himself. The Red Scorpions are known for their obsession with purity, and their hatred of their enemies. Even now he has turned to Chaos, it seems that Prayd still harbours disgust for some of his former adversaries.

'And I would not suggest that Lord Huron take my account of the daemon's words unquestioningly,' Verngar replies, with a smile that exposes his pointed canines. Valthex notes the curl of Prayd's lip in response: the former Red Scorpion is aggravated by the reminder of the flaw that lurks within the gene-seed of the Angels Encarmine. 'I believe I know where the Ebon Talon is located. I will take Lord Huron's magnanimous gift of the *Macragge's Honour* and seek out this artefact, then return with it to prove my worth. Once we have it, we can unlock the secrets of the Blackstone Fortress and activate it in Lord Huron's name.' Verngar turns his attention back to the Blood Reaver. 'Think of it, my lord! With that weapon fully at our command, the Red Corsairs can join Abaddon's crusade with a demonstration of our *own* power!'

Huron frowns, and studies the map of the galaxy as though it holds the key to his decision. Valthex glances at Verngar, but the Apostate's face is beyond his ability to read. He looks eager, but to what end? Valthex does not believe that this will truly be done for Huron's glory, despite Verngar's protests.

'I called you here to receive your counsel,' Huron rasps, looking around at his assembled officers. 'I will have it. Only a fool does not listen to his advisors. Valthex, your thoughts?'

'This tale of the Ebon Talon is a thin thread to follow,' Valthex replies, choosing his words with care. 'Prayd is correct – the daemon may be misleading us for any number of reasons. The Warmaster has called, and we should answer. We need not follow blindly, but can we afford to have stood apart if he is successful?' He extends one arm of the Indynabula Array, the ancient and arcane servo-mechanical system that was one of the relics of the Astral Claws, and which came to him when he became Master of the Forge, and uses it to indicate the white blob that represents Terra. 'The Imperium has wronged all of us, in one manner or another. We should join the strike towards its heart.'

Huron nods, and his eyes meet Valthex's with understanding. 'Well said, old friend. Verngar, I have heard your suggestion, and I presume you stand by it.'

'I do, Lord Huron,' Verngar replies smoothly.

'Turazan,' Huron says, turning to the warpsmith. 'What say you?'

'Your thoughts on the problems posed in overcoming the machine-spirit of the *Macragge's Honour* are very perceptive, Lord Huron,' Turazan says. 'The ship could become the jewel of your armada, but it cannot yet be fully trusted. Perhaps this errand would allow more time to subdue its rebellious systems, without requiring it to be used in combat against Imperial forces. Imagine if we were able to join the Warmaster, not only with an active Blackstone Fortress at our command, but also a ship of the power of the *Macragge's Honour*? It would come close to rivalling the power of a vessel like the *Conqueror* or the *Iron Blood*, even the *Vengeful Spirit* itself.'

'You would recommend Verngar pursues this artefact even if it proves to be nothing but a daemon's tale, simply to get more time in breaking the ship to our will?' Huron asks. Valthex notes that he says 'our', not 'his', but the Alchemancer has no illusions whose will Verngar wishes the *Macragge's Honour* to recognise.

Turazan spreads his hands. 'A venture with two purposes may at least accomplish one, Lord Huron.'

'Hnh,' Huron grunts, and swings his ravaged face towards the next of his commanders. 'Prayd. You distrust the daemon's words. What would you advise?'

'The Despoiler is lost to the Ruinous Powers,' Oneius Prayd says bluntly, with a challenging glare at Garlon Souleater. 'He will sacrifice any and all to achieve his goals, and so he cannot be trusted. Warmaster or not, he has no claim over us. Ignore the Fateweaver's web of lies, and if the Apostate does not feel he can trust his vessel in combat, then let him abandon it and take another.' Prayd jabs one armoured finger at the hololith. 'We should strike here.'

'Chogoris?' Huron asks, and Valthex can hear the intrigue in his master's voice. 'An interesting target, Prayd.'

'The Imperium is stretched and under threat, and the White Scars are no different,' Prayd declares viciously. 'Hitting a Chapter home world will allow us to seize a wealth of materiel and gene-seed, and the fact it belongs to a First Founding

Chapter will remind others of who we are and what we can do. Not only that,' he adds, 'but the Warmaster cannot object to some of the Imperium's greatest defenders being pinned down and slaughtered while he drives for Terra, even if it is not at his specific order. We aid his cause, but for our own gain.' The former Red Scorpion turns his smile on Turazan. 'A venture with two purposes, as you said.'

'Valid points,' Huron concedes. 'Garrix?'

'Chogoris,' the headsman responds immediately, to Valthex's surprise. 'We fight an enemy of our choosing, in a manner of our choosing – not an option we can rely on with Abaddon.'

Huron nods. 'And Garlon?'

The Souleater appears to be studying the hololith intently, but for all Valthex knows, the sorcerer could be communing with deities behind the faceplate of his helm.

'There are many powerful relics and artefacts in the galaxy,' Garlon says finally. 'It is possible that this Ebon Talon does not exist. It is certainly possible that it does not, in fact, hold the key to activating the Blackstone Fortress. However, that does not mean that it might not have other uses that could be ascertained with study.' His helmet turns towards Verngar. 'If the Apostate believes he knows the location of such an item, let him retrieve it. If he is successful, we shall see what we can make of it.'

Valthex holds his tongue, but watches Huron carefully. He has been left stranded in his support for Abaddon, and the majority consensus so far is that Verngar should be allowed to proceed. Huron Blackheart can of course overrule them all... until the day that he cannot. Valthex does not think that this is that day, but he knows the prospect cannot be far from the Blood Reaver's mind.

'Very well,' Huron says. 'Verngar, you appear to have support for your idea. Take the *Macragge's Honour* and see to it. Only the *Macragge's Honour*,' he adds, as Verngar's face splits into a smile and he begins to bow. 'The rest of the ships you returned with, and the warriors within them, will join Prayd and Garrix as they prepare for the attack on Chogoris.'

'Lord Huron,' the Apostate protests, 'those are *my* forces!'

'Then you had best complete your errand quickly, before their loyalties begin to shift!' Huron rasps. 'You have your chance to prove yourself, Verngar, and the mightiest ship at our disposal – surely you don't need an entire war fleet as well?'

'No, Lord Huron,' Verngar says, but Valthex can see the calculations going on behind the Apostate's eyes. He clearly comes to a conclusion, and whatever that conclusion is, it does not involve directly challenging Huron's authority here and now, for he holds his tongue.

'Turazan, if you wish to see to the *Macragge's Honour*, then you may do so,' Huron continues. 'Garlon, you will remain on New Badab for now, with Valthex.'

'Lord Huron,' Garlon Souleater begins, 'I will have more time to investigate the artefact if I accompany–'

'I have given you your orders, sorcerer,' Huron cuts him off. 'Do you question them?' The air on his shoulders shimmers, and the form of the Hamadrya appears. It has stubs of feather protruding from its skin this time, and a hooked beak that looks made to tear flesh, but the paws on which it scurries down Huron's arm and hops onto the edge of the hololith table are distinctly simian. It sits up onto its hind legs and chitters, fixing Garlon with its enormous black eyes.

If Garlon is disturbed by the appearance of his lord's familiar, he does not show it: he does not recoil, and his expression is, of course, impossible to see. He merely inclines his head.

'Of course not, my lord.'

'Then be about your business,' Huron growls, and his assembled commanders begin to make for the door. As Valthex turns to follow, Huron speaks again. 'Not you, Forgemaster.'

He halts, and waits. Garlon is last out, and once the door has slid shut behind him, the two former Astral Claws are alone. Not even Huron's huscarls are here: they wait outside.

'You have concerns, old friend,' Huron observes, continuing his study of the hololith.

'I do, lord,' Valthex replies, glad that he has been held back for this rather than some imagined slight or betrayal. He has faith in Huron, but the presence of the Hamadrya is a reminder that he does not truly know what his former Chapter Master is any more, or what might be whispering inside his head. 'Verngar is ambitious.'

'Good,' Huron grunts. 'I value ambition. I will not have the Corsairs sitting and sulking inside the Maelstrom like the First Legions have camped in the Eye of Terror for the last ten millennia.'

'He has already taken the *Macragge's Honour*, lord,' Valthex says. 'Despite his failure at securing Guilliman, that is still a grand prize, and he will not be short of warriors rallying to his banner.'

'Hence why I am sending the majority of them with Prayd and Garrix,' Huron points out. 'Verngar will find it hard to consolidate a power base when most of them are bleeding the White Scars.'

'If he finds this Ebon Talon, what is to say that he will return it to you?' Valthex demands. 'I appreciate that you are having Garlon remain here, to prevent Verngar from uncovering its secrets, but the Apostate may seek his own route to power by appealing to the gods directly. Assuming the Blackstone Fortress is no longer being fought over by the Neverborn, he may return there and attempt to activate it. If he manages that, your position could be under serious threat.'

'I'm aware of this, Valthex,' Huron says, and the Hamadrya scampers back up his arm onto his shoulders, from where it peers at the Alchemancer with an unwavering gaze. 'And should it come to that, I will deal with it. However, I have a solution for the shorter term.'

The Blood Reaver smiles, dead lips parting to reveal pointed teeth.

'I will be going with him.'

SIX

The tarellian kneels before Huron's throne and raises its fist above its head. Behind it, ranks of its – kin? Followers? Huron neither knows nor particularly cares – mirror its gesture. Barking, coughing sounds issue forth from reptilian snouts as they begin to utter their oath of allegiance. The tarellians hate the Imperium, and are intelligent enough to realise that although Huron was human once, he no longer has any love for the civilisation that spawned him.

Huron waits. Tarellians take their oath of allegiance seriously, and are capable fighters and renowned mercenaries. This newly arrived warband of several hundred of the scaled aliens will make a useful addition to the forces he is sending to attack Chogoris. They can die fighting the Imperium, as is their wish, and in doing so will leave his Space Marines free to engage higher priority targets.

'Lord Huron.'

The voice over his comm-bead is that of Armenneus Valthex. Huron grunts in irritation. The tarellians will not take kindly to any sign that he is not giving their oath his full attention, and although they would not survive any attempt to exact revenge for his perceived disrespect, it would be a waste of both resources and time on the Blood Reaver's behalf. On the other hand, Valthex would not contact him unless it was something important.

'What?' Huron mutters, not breaking eye contact with the tarellian leader.

'The Macragge's Honour *is being very casual about it, but it is breaking orbit.'*

Huron does not bother asking Valthex if he is sure. The Master of the Forge possesses a towering intellect, and an inherent head for numbers and data. If he has noticed a change in the orbit of Verngar's ship and has mentioned it, then it is significant enough for his conclusions to be sound.

Verngar was unable to provide coordinates for the planet on which he claims the Ebon Talon is located, so the *Spectre of Ruin* will have to match the *Macragge's Honour* move for move within the immaterium as Verngar engages in whatever process he has for navigation. If Verngar slips into the warp before Huron is ready to follow...

Huron focuses on the tarellian leader. He knows these aliens well enough to have a handle on some of their customs, and their oath is barely begun. They have to recite their lineage and the names of each member of their force, so that they are all held to the same vow. Then they have to list the enemies they will fight, and those whom they will not. The fact that Huron has little understanding of their growling is immaterial: the oath is for them, not for him as such. They are honourable, to a certain value of the word, and ferocious.

And expendable.

Huron holds up the Tyrant's Claw, palm outwards and fingers spread, to silence the tarellians. He knows what will follow, and he is correct: the xenos rise to their feet, their guttural oaths disappearing into snarls and growls as – according to their beliefs – their offer of allegiance is disrespected and thrown back into their faces. Projectile weapons are unslung and readied, blades are drawn, and devices the purpose of which Huron is not entirely sure begin to shimmer.

The tarellian leader opens its mouth to roar the order to attack.

Huron activates the heavy flamer set into the palm of the Tyrant's Claw, and a gout of flaming promethium jets out with a roar to embrace a teardrop-shaped chunk of the first eight ranks of xenos.

There is no point explaining the situation; the tarellians will neither understand nor care. More importantly, Huron Blackheart does not beg the understanding of lesser beings. Had the tarellians fallen silent, they would have lived. Instead they valued their supposed honour more highly than they respected his authority, or valued their own lives. They have made their choice, and now they must live with it. Or more accurately, die with it.

Huron snatches up his power axe and wades into the mass of howling aliens, his face split in a death's-head rictus of a grin. This is not his wish or his purpose, for these deaths will neither affect the Imperium one jot, nor increase his own power. However, it is a necessity.

Besides, he was born to kill. For all of the Imperium's faults and failings, it breeds killers very well. Its folly lies in trying to keep them on too short a leash, and in telling itself that the Adeptus Astartes are anything more or less than murderers.

'To *Bloodstrike*!' he bellows, as his four huscarls close in on his position. 'I must get to the *Spectre of Ruin* immediately!'

The tarellians are doomed, and they know it, but they will not go down without a fight. One of them, a hissing, blazing wreck, barrels out of the press and hurls itself at Huron with outstretched claws that are already blackening from the fire consuming it. Huron swats it away with a backhanded blow from the Tyrant's Claw, and it lands in a screaming heap somewhere behind his right shoulder. Huron uses the motion as the backswing to flow immediately into a punch with the same weapon, which pulverises another tarellian's torso and sends it flying back into its fellows, then pivots and brings his power axe down in a strike that bisects a third alien along the diagonal.

Huron Blackheart is a wreck of a being, held together by spite and sorcery and mechanical ingenuity, and his movements no longer hold the same speed that they once did, but that does not mean he is any less deadly in combat. For all that his weapons are hardly precision tools, his strikes are placed with the care of centuries of experience, his steps are guided by the swirling awareness of the warp, and his strength is as ferocious as it ever was. He cannot avoid all the blows his enemies launch at him, but few land flush: they skitter off the rounded surface of a pauldron, land on an armour plate instead of piercing a joint, or are parried just when it seems his misshapen skull is going to finally be split in two.

Huron catches the blade of a double-handed tarellian axe in the palm of the Tyrant's Claw and lashes out with a kick, splintering whatever serves the xenos as ribs and sending it sprawling to the ground. He then readjusts his grip to seize the haft, and swings downwards to bury the blade in the tarellian's head. It dies immediately with only a few reflexive twitches and Huron strides on past it, his pace unwavering and his advance unstoppable.

'*Bloodstrike* is preparing for launch, lord,' Tagron growls as he punches an alien in half with the massive power fist of his Terminator armour: a weapon of lesser lineage than the Tyrant's Claw, but no less deadly. His combi-bolter chatters, and kills two more. 'They will be ready by the time we reach them.'

'Good,' Huron grunts, and cuts down another tarellian. 'Signal the *Spectre*. They are to shadow the *Macragge's Honour*, and are to be ready to translate as soon as we board.'

'The Apostate is seeking to get ahead of you, lord?' asks the huscarl on Huron's other side. 'The filthy traitor should have his soul stripped out of him!'

'We're all traitors, Rafken, or have you forgotten?' Huron chuckles. 'I didn't tell Verngar my plans, and besides, I still have a use for him.' He sways back from a blade that stabs at his face, grabs the arm that wields it with the Tyrant's Claw, and twists the offending limb clean off with a swift snapping motion. The tarellian staggers backwards howling as its blue-green blood spurts out, and Huron takes its head with his power axe. 'I'll let you know when the situation changes.'

The full-throated bark of boltguns fills the air. It is no longer Huron and his bodyguards fighting alone against the mass of xenos in his throne room; the honour guards stationed outside have rushed in through the doors and turned their weapons on the tarellians. Huron keeps at least one member of each of the Chapters who have come into his service lining the approach to his throne room, partly to emphasise his power and influence to those who come to petition him, and partly because it amuses him to station old rivals and enemies next to each other. Now, however, they act as one, and although it does not change the result of the combat, it greatly speeds it. Within a matter of seconds there are no tarellians left standing, and the air is filled with the stink of cordite and misty droplets of xenos blood.

'I want this cleaned up!' Huron barks, stepping forward over the bodies. He has no interest in who does it or how, whether it is work teams of slaves or a sorcerer who has some use for the dead flesh, so long as his throne room is back to its former glory by the time he returns. He knows it will be: no one wishes to displease the Tyrant of New Badab. 'And I want *Bloodstrike* at capacity before we take off!'

Tagron barks the orders over the vox as they make for the grand stairway that leads up to the roof of the Palace of Thorns. Lesser warriors will rush to obey, for the glory of accompanying the Blood Reaver is one they all crave.

Huron stamps upwards, silently cursing the Imperium with every step, for he has not been free of suffering for nearly a century. The indoctrination he underwent as an Astral Claws neophyte enabled him to ignore pain that would incapacitate an unaugmented human, and the work of Valthex and Garreon numbed it further, but there is no way around the fact that nearly half his body was vaporised or cooked. The places where his flesh interfaces with the biomechanics are a permanent raw wound that continually throbs in his mind. Almost worse are the phantom pains that still plague him, despite the limbs in question being gone and wholly replaced with prosthetics.

Lesser minds would have snapped under the unending agony, or would have sought more and more desperate bargains to ease it. Huron knows well enough that some of Nurgle's devotees feel no pain, those of Slaanesh consider it a form of ecstasy and use it to push themselves to new heights; he knows that the followers of Khorne would draw power from it in the form of battle rage, and acolytes of Tzeentch would be able to alter their bodies so that the pain was banished completely. All he needs to do is conduct the correct rituals, utter the correct incantations...

However, Huron Blackheart is no god's puppet, and he will not let his own suffering drive him to make deals that he will regret. This pain reminds him of how the Imperium betrayed him, so he will keep it. It is a part of him; without it, he might forget some of who he is.

He continues to climb, his face locked into a scowl.

The roof of the Palace of Thorns is a seamless blend of vanity and brutality. Massive banners bearing the icon of the Red Corsairs stand tall, snapping in the warp-tainted winds of New Badab, and gold and jewels glint in wordless testimony to the riches accrued by a century of raiding. However, power sits here too: the big guns of which Huron is so fond are placed in a defensive array he devised himself, ensuring that all approaches are covered by overlapping fields of fire. Any force descending from the multi-hued skies, or advancing overland, will find itself torn apart by macrocannon shells and twin-linked turbo-lasers, to say nothing of the smaller Hydra anti-aircraft batteries, lascannon emplacements, mortars and sundry other weapons of war. Massive void shield generators that once belonged to a starship can bring up a protective field of energy if the palace is threatened with bombardment, but that has never happened. None dare to challenge Huron here; or at least, none that have proved capable of finding him.

There are landing pads up here too, and on one of them squats a truly ancient machine the colour of dried blood. *Bloodstrike* is a Stormbird, one of the mighty Legiones Astartes transports that dates back to the time of the Great Crusade. It once belonged to the Word Bearers, but Huron took it from their grasp a couple of decades ago to serve as his personal transport. It is a corrupted thing, with the engine intakes and weapon barrels warped into the shape of howling maws, and its ceramite skin weeps black blood when damaged, but corruption can be a boon when navigating the Maelstrom. Besides, it still flies, and it still functions, and that is all that Huron demands.

In the twisted shadow of its cockpit stand thirty renegade Space Marines. Huron takes them in as he advances towards them. All of them are in the colours of the Red Corsairs, of course, but he can pick out idiosyncrasies which betray their previous allegiances. That helmetless head has the pale skin and black eyes of a former Night Lord; the warrior beside him carries a gladius which certainly came from an Ultramarine, and Huron suspects the owner was once of the same Chapter. A champion leading one of the squads even bears the eye of Horus on his breast, albeit cracked and shattered; not even the original members of the Black Legion are always content to follow the Warmaster, and it looks like one of those ancient warriors decided he preferred his prospects under Huron's rule.

Most of those assembled, however, are Red Corsairs in truth. Some were Astral Claws, and Huron notes the talons that have replaced fingers, or the horns that spiral out from temples or strike upwards from the crown of the head, and which make helmets useless. Others have never been anything except Red Corsairs: youths snatched from planets under the swirling skies of the Maelstrom, or worlds in the Imperium near its borders, and who survived the harrowing ascension process. Some have Astral Claws gene-seed, and some have that which has been looted from other Chapters over the decades, but they are united under his leadership.

Behind these troops are other, more specialised warriors. Six Raptors skulk there, twisted avian shapes that were once

Assault Marines, whose jump packs became welded to them and for whom the thrill of flight and striking the enemy from above has become an all-consuming desire. Huron also makes out three mighty Obliterators, hulking brutes whose bodies have been both ravaged and blessed by the attentions of Turazan and his kin in the Dark Mechanicum. Their forms are constantly shifting quietly, as though components and cabling are sliding beneath their skin and integrating into their armour, then disappearing once more. At the moment such changes are slight, but Huron knows that once battle is joined their flesh will erupt and re-form into the muzzles of mighty cannons capable of shredding their foes. Even a force as mighty as his does not contain many such behemoths, and their presence here is a welcome one.

He smiles. The *Spectre of Ruin* will not carry the hordes he might have hoped as he follows Verngar's questionable lead, but he will not be weak. Should the Ebon Talon exist, Huron doubts very much whether it will be a simple matter to take it from its resting place. He might well face opposition as he tries to do so.

He might even face opposition from his own underling.

'Board!' he snaps, and the assembled Corsairs oblige with alacrity. Huron follows them up the ramp, the centre of a cross with his massive huscarls at the points.

'Now get us into orbit!' he bellows at the pilot, a half-flesh, half-metal creature called Carazzalan. Once upon a time, two Word Bearers sat there, welded into place by millennia of servitude in the warp. Huron had Garlon and Turazan combine their knowledge to have the scions of Lorgar ripped out physically and spiritually, and replaced with one of his own Mechanicum adepts who was only too happy to have their spirit joined to such a venerable war machine.

Bloodstrike's engines fire up, and it jerks into the air like a scalded animal. Huron grunts, and holds onto Rafken's massive pauldron for momentary support. His Hamadrya swirls into existence for a moment, chittering excitedly, then fades away again. Huron can sense its eagerness to return to the real warp, the realm from whence it originally came, not this halfway place where the immaterium and realspace slide past each other.

It won't get the chance, if he has anything to say about it. Huron has no interest in having the *Spectre of Ruin* overrun by daemons, half his crew developing an insatiable bloodlust, or any other complications of warp travel. One day, perhaps, Huron Blackheart will find himself adrift in the warp without the defence of a Geller field, and on that day he will deal with the predators that will come for him in whatever manner he can. They may even learn that he has teeth of his own, for the warp is not the same foreign realm for Huron that it is for most other mortals.

For now, though, he has his rule to maintain.

SEVEN

'Give me an update!' Huron snarls as he strides onto the bridge of the *Spectre of Ruin*. 'Where is the *Macragge's Honour*? Have they jumped yet?'

'No, lord,' the Master of Auspex replies. 'However, they are now far enough away from New Badab to make the translation safely, and from other ships to prevent them being sucked in with them. They've been moving slowly, but their intent seems clear.'

Huron grunts. Concepts like the Mandeville point have less relevance in these parts of the Maelstrom, where they already wade in the shallows of the warp in any case, but there are still some constraints. The warp is fickle, after all, and only a fool takes liberties with it.

He scans the displays until he finds the point of light that signifies the former Ultramarines ship, then triangulates that to locate it with his own eyes against the background of the warp-tinted void. There are many drive trails out there, but Huron has centuries of experience at interpreting tactical schematics into three-dimensional pictures.

'And so the Apostate attempts to slide out of sight with no announcement of his departure, like a thief in the night,' he rasps. 'Hardly in keeping with his character. I wonder if this is because he expects me to follow? But it matters not. Are we ready to translate?'

'Aye, lord,' the reply comes back. 'Warp engines are ready to power up, and the Geller field is on standby.'

Huron nods, and turns to Tagron. 'I want a rundown of all Space Marines present on this ship, as well as any other notable assets – vehicles, mortal sorcerers and the like. Make it as complete as possible.'

'Yes, lord,' Tagron replies, and heads for the entrance to the bridge. The huscarl will find someone else to do it: there will be Mechanicum adepts somewhere who have the kind of data-compiling abilities such a task requires.

One of the very few advantages he had as an Imperial commander, Huron reflects ruefully, was that at least he had a good idea of who was under that command at any one time. There had been lists of squads and companies, with notes to highlight where battle attrition meant that this squad or that squad were under-strength, or where their designated transport had been destroyed. He knew how much ammunition was at his disposal, often to the individual shell or power pack. There was no hope of that now; even if some sort of complete headcount was achieved on the *Spectre of Ruin* before they reached their destination, he had no assurance that a clash in the depths of the ship would not claim lives before he ever had a chance to expend them in combat. And that was assuming the battle-barge itself did not absorb a few luckless souls, for some of the *Spectre*'s deepest internal holds and corridors housed hungry shadows that no light could banish.

'The followers of the Plague Lord like to count,' Huron muses, absent-mindedly reaching up one hand to scratch the Hamadrya, which coos half-words into his ear. 'Perhaps I should harness one of his minor daemons as a quartermaster.'

His voice is not loud, but a few necks stiffen across the bridge. None of the human crew are looking at him, but Huron can taste their sudden fear on the air. Devoted followers or not, few of them are sanguine about the suggestion of a daemonic presence in their midst. Their fear irritates Huron: do they not know how hard he has worked to resist the temptations dangled in front of him by greedy gods? He could have followed the path of the Word Bearers with ease; could have struck bargain after bargain, and offered up the living flesh of his followers as vessels for the Neverborn in exchange for power, insight or wisdom. One moment of dark humour is enough to turn their stomachs? He opens his mouth to snarl something, but is cut off by the auspex officer.

'Warp drive activation!' the man shouts. 'The *Macragge's Honour* is preparing to translate!'

'Match them!' Huron commands, and a moment later lights start flashing and klaxons wail as the overseers of the enginarium begin the procedure that will allow the battle-barge to slip through the fabric of reality. Huron eyes the shimmer that is starting to appear ahead of the point of light which signifies the *Macragge's Honour* in the forward viewport, just as the protective shutters begin to descend. He can only react to Verngar's moves, of course, but the *Spectre of Ruin* is as ready as it can be, and there is every possibility that the *Macragge's Honour* will still be sluggish in responding to commands coming from those it has considered enemies for ten thousand years.

'Vox from the Navigator, lord!' someone shouts. 'She needs to know our heading!'

'Tell her to follow the *Macragge's Honour*!' Huron replies, setting his feet. Blinking lumens indicate that the Geller field has activated, and so his ship is as well defended as it can be from whatever awaits them in the true warp. Huron readies his weapons anyway, because he knows better than to trust too faithfully in anything. All across the *Spectre of Ruin*, his crew and warriors will be doing whatever rituals they believe might help keep them safe from the predators of the warp. When it comes down to it, even followers of the Ruinous Powers would generally prefer to have a daemon tearing their enemies' souls apart, rather than their own.

'Translating in three, two, one...'

The klaxons hit a new note and the *Spectre of Ruin* lurches, or perhaps more accurately, the galaxy does. They shudder through their translation as the warp drive parts reality, and they dive down into the roiling mass of the empyrean. Huron can taste something like burned sugar on his tongue.

The ship's shuddering does not stop. Whatever currents it has landed in, they are violent ones. Mortals hold onto the frames of their workstations to prevent themselves from being shaken out of their seats, but Huron's huscarls stand fast as the servos in their Terminator armour react immediately to every jolt.

'Patch me through to the Navigator,' Huron instructs the vox-officer, who obliges. The Blood Reaver waits for the click that signifies his comm-bead syncing with the ship's internal communication system, then speaks. 'Navigator, can you see the *Macragge's Honour*?'

'"See" is a misnomer, lord,' the voice of Beis Fortuna replies. *'Perceiving the warp is something completely different to the act of using mortal eyes.'*

'Do not play word games with me,' Huron growls. 'I may lack one of your eyes, but I know the warp in ways you will never imagine.' Fortuna was snatched from an Imperial merchantman over thirty years ago, and although she acquiesced to serving the Red Corsairs without too many problems, she still has flashes of her own spirit now and then. Huron normally finds these mildly amusing, but he is in no mood for jests today. 'Can you *perceive* it, or not? You need to follow it, because they are the ones who know our destination.'

'Forgive my honesty, lord, but I was buying time to answer,' Fortuna says, and now Huron can hear the strain in the mutant's voice. *'I can make out the other vessel, but it is not clear to me, and the flows here are strong. If they picked the translation point then they did so poorly, if they expected me to be able to easily keep us apace with them.'*

Huron grunts. It would be just like Verngar to have his own Navigator monitor the warp before translating, then deliberately take them into rough currents where they would be hard to follow. Is the Apostate still using the Ultramarines' Navigator, or has he had time to install one of his own? Huron does not know, but it is safest to assume that everyone on the ship, and indeed the ship itself, are loyal to Verngar and will do his bidding without objection.

Of course, even that assumption is not without risk. If the other ship's Navigator is still loyal to the Imperium, there is nothing to say that they might not make some misguidedly noble decision to sacrifice themselves in order to bring the *Macragge's Honour* to ruin, and in the hope that the *Spectre* will follow it to its own doom.

'I want us shadowing that ship,' Huron tells Fortuna. 'Expect them to try to lose us. Make sure they do not.'

'Acknowledged, lord,' Fortuna replies, and the lack of any

sort of clever remark tells Huron how difficult she expects this task to be.

Navigators are a strange sort, prone to odd moods and eccentricities, and those idiosyncrasies must be tolerated – to a certain extent – if they are to be of any use. Huron hates waste: it is part of the reason he turned against the Imperium, after all. He is not the type to punish a Navigator for showing disrespect, when both he and she know that he holds her life in his hand. If Beis Fortuna cannot muster some sort of humour or wit, it is not because she fears him – although she does – but because she is concentrating as hard as she can.

There are potential alternatives, of course. There will be sorcerers aboard the *Spectre*, Astartes from the Red Corsairs' Librarius and mortals who have made their own bargains with the gods. Some of them may be able to plough through the warp in their own way, but Huron is wary of such tactics. Navigators have been bred for this purpose for millennia, and more importantly, have little use for personal gain or power once shackled to a ship. He is no tyrant to Beis Fortuna, and so he is reasonably certain that she harbours him no particular grudge that a rival could capitalise on. Sorcerers, however, are a law unto themselves, if they are allowed to be. Huron will use them as tools, but he does not relish the prospect of putting himself wholly into their hands.

Let the Navigator do her job for now. Other options can be explored if it proves necess–

'Lord, I'm losing them already. I don't know if it's their intention, or even if they're aware of us, but the tides here are obscuring them and causing our paths to diverge.'

Huron feels the ship shudder as they hit a patch of warp turbulence: or perhaps, more alarmingly, something hits the ship.

'If I knew our destination I could find us an alternative route,

one that won't see us shaken to pieces, but to follow them blindly will see us lost.'

Huron turns with a snarl. 'Get a sorcerer up here!'

The sorcerer's name is Nalik, and he is a mortal, or was once, at least. His robes bear the sigils of Tzeentch, and the Changer of Ways, as is his wont, has warped his servant's form. The right hand that clutches Nalik's staff has nine digits, each with nine knuckles, and the left has shifted into a tentacular appendage with razor-sharp spines down the back, while each of the fang-edged mouths underneath contains a tiny, baleful eye. Nalik's own eyes burn a deep, cobalt blue, with only the slenderest slash of a black pupil cutting across them, and the cowl of his robe is pushed upwards and outwards by the stubs of horns that are beginning to protrude from his brow.

He smiles at Huron, revealing large, sharp teeth of glossy black carbon, and drops to one knee with a flourish. 'Lord Huron. How may I serve you?'

Huron impales him on the fingers of the Tyrant's Claw.

Nalik gasps as the energy-shrouded metal enters his flesh, and begins to draw on the powers of his patron to defend himself, but Huron is no capricious champion to be undone by his own hubris. The Hamadrya shimmers into existence on his shoulder and scampers down his arm, and the magic that Nalik was desperately calling on dissipates into Huron's familiar, which chitters in excitement. As the Hamadrya drinks in the energy of the dying sorcerer, Huron feels his own awareness grow, just as he intended. He was no psyker in his former life, but he has found the warp more open to his mind since he made the bargains that anchored him back into the shell of his own ravaged flesh.

Further deals with the Ruinous Powers made on his own

behalf are something he wishes to avoid. Using the stolen power of another, however, carries far less risk.

Huron raises the Tyrant's Claw and brings Nalik's body with it. The sorcerer cries out in anguish as his impaled form is hoisted off the deck, and his blood drizzles downwards, but with his magic being stolen from him he can do nothing except strike weakly at Huron's head with his staff. Huron catches the blow without needing to think about it, wrenches the tool from its owner's grasp, and breaks it across Nalik's face.

'Die quietly, wretch,' the Blood Reaver rasps. Not even the favour of Tzeentch can help Nalik avoid doing just that, and within half a minute he is slumped unmoving on the end of Huron's talons.

Huron lowers his arm, and Nalik's corpse slides off to land wetly on the deck of the *Spectre of Ruin*'s bridge. The crew have been paying the entire affair little mind. That is partly because they are concentrating on their jobs, trying to keep the ship under control so far as possible in the turmoil that surrounds them, but mainly because they are no strangers to violent death. Service to the Red Corsairs guarantees that: their only concern is ensuring that their masters have no reason to inflict it on them.

'Now,' Huron says, taking up the longer half of Nalik's staff and tracing shapes through the sorcerer's blood. 'Let us see what we can find.'

Power flows into his glyphs as he bends the warp to his whims, guided by the Hamadrya's soft cooing. The creature forms no words he can understand, but somehow the meaning of its noises flows into his brain and down his arm, and yet he has not become something else's puppet. Huron Blackheart is still his own man, and he has not yet overreached himself.

The final line is drawn, and he closes his eyes, concentrating. Then he sends his consciousness outwards, fortified and buffered by the power he has stolen from Nalik.

His mind is assailed almost instantaneously, for this is no mere Adeptus Mechanicus mining station through which he is projecting, but the hostile currents of the warp itself. Predators lurk within it: predators who have already been drawn to the contents of his ship. The followers of Chaos are not always the most tempting morsels for those who lurk in the immaterium, for bargains are made and power is wrought to provide protection beyond that of a simple Geller field, but that does not mean that they can traverse its currents with impunity. Huron feels the scrape of psychic talons down the armoured flanks of his mind, and senses slavering jaws searching for any chink in his mental armour that will allow the beasts to crack his defences open and get to the tender meat beneath.

He grits his teeth and presses on. He has no weapon with which he can drive the beasts back, no prayer to the Emperor he can shout to clear his path. He simply hardens his will and keeps going, ignoring the pain, ignoring the distractions, ignoring everything that does not matter to him.

He has decades of experience.

He is certain that he does not perceive his surroundings as Beis Fortuna does: he cannot see the ebb and flow of the warp currents; he cannot perceive the dangers on which his ship might founder, or become becalmed forever. What he can do, however, is find the faint spoor of his quarry. He knows Verngar the Apostate, and he can even sense the lingering taint of the Ultramarines vessel. Somewhere out there, in the middle of the ravening storm that surrounds him, his mind's eye sees the faint light of their existence, try though they might to evade him. He cannot guide the *Spectre of Ruin* after them, because he cannot make out the routes they can take. But then again, he does not need to.

'Navigator,' he hisses through his teeth. 'I will give you our heading, and you will find a way to get us there. Is that understood?'

'It is, Lord Huron,' Fortuna replies. She does not ask how he has done this. She knows him well enough by now to accept that what he says is true, and also that she is unlikely to want to learn the details.

'Good,' Huron says, and spits onto Nalik's corpse, where his saliva slowly begins to eat away at the sorcerer's face. 'Then let us begin.'

EIGHT

Huron.

The voice is deep and dark, sweet and foul, like honeyed effluent dripping onto the tongue. It is a voice that oozes under doors and seeps through walls. It is a voice that pools in the shadows and avoids the light; not out of fear, but to taunt. It is a voice that is always just behind the ear, just around the corner, just out of sight. It is a voice that is simultaneously fingernails down bone, salt in a wound, and feathers brushed across sunburn. It is a voice that enters through the eyes and cuts skin from the inside.

Blood Reaver!

Huron focuses on the shifting blur that is his image of Verngar the Apostate and his stolen vessel, and ignores it.

Why do you struggle so, Huron? Why do you limit yourself?

'Ten degrees to starboard, fifteen below us,' Huron grates. He is not talking to the voice.

'Acknowledged, lord,' Beis Fortuna replies into his ear. She sounds less strained now she has a heading, rather than having to keep track of the *Macragge's Honour* herself. Huron tells her in which direction they should be heading, and she finds a course to take them there. It is nowhere near as easy for her as having a set destination, but it's far less difficult than it was, because Huron has taken on the hard part.

He could have used a sorcerer, of course, but Huron Blackheart detests being beholden to others. And besides, he has never been one to hang back from things.

Your connection to your quarry is tenuous, Huron. Your understanding of the warp is still so **limited–**

Huron growls as a splash of nausea-inducing colour washes over his awareness. Reaching out into the immaterium with his mind is like holding his hand steady in a fast-flowing stream of irritant chemicals, the constant stinging and itching threatening to derail his concentration. The main difference is that if he wavers, the irritants will immediately transform into a tide of acid that will either dissolve him completely, or at the very least leave him an unrecognisable ruin of what he was.

Huron has already been through such an experience once. No one who looked upon the proud features of Lugft Huron, Chapter Master of the Astral Claws, would have considered he could have been the same being as the scarred, half-dead Blood Reaver. He knows he still has a lot left to lose, but his determination is all the greater for it.

I can help you. Let me help you.

The same blandishments, the same temptations. The powers of Chaos have fewer weapons at their disposal to corrupt Space Marines, because there are fewer things that Space Marines want. Huron has no carnal desires, nor does he take any pleasure in food or drink. His bioengineered constitution still metabolises narcotics and toxins fast enough that anything potent enough to affect him would be a threat to his very existence. Nor does Huron have any great desire for material wealth: the opulence of the Palace of Thorns is a functional affair, designed to impress those who are impressed by such things, and remind them of his might – for those more interested in practical matters, the size of his forces, the peerless design of his stronghold and the immense weapons mounted upon it will suffice.

The only thing Huron desires – the only thing he has ever desired – is power, but even then, he does not desire power for power's sake. Huron has always been a general, not a monarch. When he ruled Badab, he desired power to defend the Imperium effectively against raiders from the Maelstrom. Since the Imperium turned on him, he has desired power to take revenge and show them how foolish they were to make him into an enemy, instead of letting him fight their enemies for them.

He desires power so he can most efficiently perform the tasks he wishes to achieve. That is the only bait that can lure him, and so that is how the hook is set, again and again.

You are weak.

I am strong enough for this, Huron replies. The voice of his mind is not the oratorical boom of his old life, but the halting, clicking rasp he possesses now. Huron does not yearn for former days.

You are not, the voice insists. ***You will fail. You will lose your quarry and you will fail. You will lose your power. You will lose your influence and your position. You will be cast down, your strength revealed as a brittle shell.***

In his mind, Huron sees images as the voice speaks. He sees Verngar holding something triumphantly aloft, although the details of the object are obscured; he sees Red Corsairs chanting the Apostate's name and kneeling before him; he sees Stormfiend flashing towards him, its wielder's face twisted in rage.

I can help you.

'Course change,' Huron says aloud. 'Now five degrees to port, ten degrees below.'

'Acknowledged, lord.'

They're slipping away from you. I can make you stronger.

Who are you? Huron demands. There is a pause before the voice replies.

I am–

Irrelevant! Huron snaps, and laughs as he senses the voice recoil in surprise, and rapidly growing anger. *Do you understand me, you pathetic shred of spirit? You have nothing,* nothing, *that can interest me. You claim you can make me stronger, but you seek to make me a servant, and I. Do. Not.* Serve. *I have made my bargains with far greater powers, and I need nothing from the likes of* you.

When the voice returns, it is no longer smooth and insidious, but a roar of primordial rage that hurls its thoughts against Huron's mental barriers like bolter shells fired into a wall.

Insolent mortal! You taste a sliver of power and think yourself great – you gain a morsel of knowledge and consider yourself wise! You parade the paltry gifts for which you bartered as though you are anything other than a dead man kept alive by the will of others!

The wall of Huron's will holds, despite the impacts, although the Hamadrya whimpers and cowers as the wash of hatred flows over the link they share.

You are a moment of whimsy, a fleeting curiosity whose time will pass, and when it does…

The voice subsides a little, and Huron can taste the dark amusement floating at its surface.

Then I will be waiting, little one. I will see how loud dead flesh can scream.

'Directly ahead,' Huron says, and smiles at the momentary frustration he senses from the voice – frustration that even now, he is not giving it his full attention. 'Eight degrees up.'

You cannot hide from the truth, Huron. You are nothing.

Take all the work of others away, Huron replies fiercely, *and what is left?*

A dead man.

A dead man who is still more than you will ever be, and has achieved more than you ever can. You are a slave to the whims of your patron, whoever you are, but I am no tool. He flexes the fingers of the Tyrant's Claw. *I am the hand that wields the tool.*

You are nothing but a pawn in the games of the gods, as are all mortals.

Then it must be the will of the gods for me to tell you to go and eat aeldari filth, Huron snarls. *Cease bothering me, Neverborn, and return to your pathetic dreams of realspace.*

The voice quietens. Huron does not believe that the intellect behind it has truly heeded him, but it appears to have decided that it cannot further its purposes with him at this time, and that is all he required. If they cannot use you, and cannot destroy you, the creatures of the empyrean have little patience for dealing with mortals. Perhaps it has marked him in some sense; perhaps, when the time finally comes for his soul to be offered up to the warp, this being will seek some part of it on which to wreak petty revenge.

That is no concern. Huron long ago accepted the price of his actions, and this has no impact on his calculations. Besides, he still has coin that will draw forth favour, should he choose to barter with it.

'Three degrees to starboard,' he tells Beis Fortuna, 'and keep it level.' He smiles. He cannot see the *Macragge's Honour* wallowing through the warp's currents, as such, but he knows what his hunter's senses are telling him. 'We're gaining on them.'

NINE

Griza Dallax had never left the *Spectre of Ruin*. She saw little reason to, since she had not been instructed to by Huron, and had little desire to experience the surface of a warp-tainted world for herself. She wonders at that, for surely the prospect of such a novel experience should be of great interest to an adept of the Mechanicus? Even though her interests and specialities lie with battle automata, has anyone else ever properly evaluated such a place? Let alone one that is also the stronghold of one of the Imperium's bitterest former sons. She could have gathered vital data about the nature of Huron's defences.

But to what purpose? She has no way of communicating such intelligence to any forces that could make use of it. Even if she did, is she not now tainted, at least by association? She knows that she would view with great distrust any information provided to her by someone who had travelled with the Red Corsairs, no matter how briefly. She has already profaned the appearance of her charges with blood, and the fact that it was the blood of traitors is of no great comfort to her: there is a difference between the stains that can accrue as a natural part of battle, and deliberate anointing. She has not performed the ritual cleansings, both physical and of the machine-spirit; she has potentially corrupted her automata just by using non-sanctified arcflood outflows.

She has betrayed the Omnissiah with her actions, if not her intentions. She should, by the standards of everything she learned as an adept, destroy herself to avoid further corruption.

And yet...

Who is she to decide whether she is beyond redemption, Griza Dallax wonders. Should she not still be trying to return to the arms of the Mechanicus, should such an opportunity present itself? Then, if she is considered to have fallen too far from the teachings of the Omnissiah, appropriate measures can be taken: measures that would be no more final than any action she could take herself, here and now. And then at least her former colleagues would once more have access to her kastelans, which would otherwise remain in the hands of these renegades for their systems to be preyed upon, taken apart, or overridden by the first heretek to discover them unprotected. That was another consideration when deciding whether or not to venture down to New Badab: who knew what manner of foul being awaited there, who would seek to take her robots from her? At least on the *Spectre of Ruin* she has a greater chance of avoiding the attention of the majority of these renegades.

Huron Blackheart, may all his systems fail, was right about one thing: she can always choose to die tomorrow.

She has stayed mainly on the underdecks, roving the corridors and passageways, never remaining in one spot for too long. She and her charges are more than a match for any of the scum they encounter down here, for this is the realm of work gangs, menials and the twisted wretches who have either fled from what passes as society on the ship, or were never part of it. Should she set up any form of permanent residence, however, she fears that word of her presence might get out to those who would seek to take what she has, and have some chance of doing so. She can find appropriate nutrition for herself, and has made a note of suitable charging points for her automata. That is all she requires.

She notices when the *Spectre* translates into the warp, of course. Even down here, in the realms where few of the souls present have much individual worth to the ship's masters, the alarms still sound as the warp engines activate and the Geller field powers up. Prayers are still uttered and symbols are still traced in the air, but the prayers are not to the Emperor or the Omnissiah, and the symbols are not that of the aquila or the sacred cogwheel. It is neither a smooth translation, nor a smooth voyage afterwards. The *Spectre* takes jolts of what must be staggering power, given the size of the ship, and Griza hears wails of trepidation. Even the servants of the warp still fear its attentions, it appears: she wonders if they fear it more, due to some familiarity with its nature.

She advances out of the shadows, backed by her looming bodyguards, and the leader of a work gang turns towards her. He is mutated, a corrupted form of humanity with bony spurs jutting through his purple-tinged skin at the knees, elbows, knuckles and brow-ridge. He raises his whip as a threat to whoever is approaching him from behind, then lowers it again as he takes in the sight in front of him. He does not kneel, but the aggression drains away, leaving only the tension of fear. He will run if he feels threatened, but he will not fight.

Griza experiences a rush of chemicals in her bloodstream, and realises that she is feeling pleasure. She finds it gratifying that this man – this heretic traitor – is intimidated by her, and will offer no challenge to her authority: the authority she possesses through nothing more complicated than perceived force of arms.

'Where are we headed?' she demands. The mutant barks a harsh laugh, and she catches a flicker of an overlarge tongue behind his teeth.

'Who knows?' he retorts. 'Who cares? S'not our concern.'

Griza buzzes, which is her vocal equivalent of a disapproving tut for a regular human. 'Who knows, indeed?' She waits, but it appears he has taken her utterance as rhetorical. 'I desire to know. Who can provide me with this information?'

'One of the masters could, if you're foolish enough to ask,' the mutant says, edging away from her a little. 'Or you can find a viewport and look out of it, if you're that interested.'

It appears that fear does not necessarily equate to either usefulness or respect. Griza considers her options and the likely outcomes of them for one point two eight seconds, then raises her gamma pistol.

'One of the masters, one of the masters!' the man babbles, cowering backwards and raising his arms in a useless attempt to protect his head and body. 'They're the only ones as would know!'

'You refer to one of the Heretic Astartes?' Griza queries. The overseer lowers his arms slightly, peering out at her from behind them.

'Heretic? Where in the warp's name did you get dragged up from? You're on a renegade ship, cog-girl! We serve the true powers here, not the Corpse-Emperor!'

His point is valid – there was no need to preface the word

'Astartes' with a descriptor, bearing in mind her situation – but Griza finds his tone irritating, as well as his reminder that she is surrounded by the enemies of humanity. This time her period of consideration is somewhat shorter, and ends with his skin blistering and flesh melting as her gamma pistol fires. He falls backwards with a rapidly truncated scream, dropping the whip with which he had until recently been menacing those under his command. The eyes of the work gang are all drawn to it as it slips from his fingers and skitters across the tarnished metal plates of the deck.

Griza neither says nor does anything, but simply waits. She is momentarily intrigued by this insight into the organic hierarchies of these slaves. Will any of them make the first move to seize this weapon, which to judge by their reactions is as symbolic as it is practical? Do any of them seek to wield power, or do they lack the drive or initiative for their own advancement?

After a moment of taut hesitation, they flee.

The gang moves as a group, similar to herd animals when chased by a predator, if herd animals shove and punch and kick and bite in an attempt not just to move faster, but also to delay those around them and leave a more obvious potential victim. Griza does not understand their reaction at first, because her interactions had been solely with the overseer, and she had not made any threats towards the rest. However, as her auditory sensors detect a repeated sound, she begins to understand.

She knows the sound of ceramite on metal well, because ceramite is what her kastelans are armoured in. However, her automata are not in motion; and besides, although still heavy, these footfalls are lighter and quicker than those of her robots. That can leave only one possibility.

The Red Corsairs are coming.

Griza turns and ushers her charges away, back into the shadows from whence they had emerged. She has no wish to encounter Huron's reavers, especially given the reaction of the work gang, which suggests that the Space Marines pose a threat to those who dwell on these decks. Do they hunt the menials for sport? It would be well within the parameters of behaviour that Griza has for them, and she has already decided that her own knowledge is likely to be a pale reflection of the true savagery of these heretics.

She is under no illusion that she can truly hide from the Red Corsairs: certainly not in shadows, which will be easily penetrated by the sensors of their helmets, even if not by any unclean distortions of their physiology. However, if they are hunting for sport then logic suggests that they will pursue the largest pack of prey animals – she realises that she has dehumanised the thralls in her thoughts, then pushes that thought aside with the rationalisation that as heretics, they are not to be considered as human in any case – rather than venturing into areas where there is a lower chance of success.

She rounds three corners, surrounded by her kastelans, then halts and monitors for sounds of pursuit. Echoes make clear interpretation of data difficult in any collection of tunnels or corridors, but the *Spectre of Ruin* appears to distort sound in a way that is different to other environments Griza has encountered previously. She wonders if this is because of some idiosyncrasy of construction of a Space Marine battle-barge as opposed to the Adeptus Mechanicus ships with which she is familiar; she suspects that it might in fact be a result of other, less rational causes, such as prolonged exposure to the warp. To someone who treats data as an absolute, the notion that it is being altered by unpredictable factors beyond her control is unsettling in the extreme.

Not as unsettling, however, as the realisation that she can indeed still detect the sound of footfalls, and that they appear to be tracking her.

Griza sets off again, attempting to balance speed with stealth, but while the long strides of her kastelans are more than adequate for the former, their massive weight means they are sorely lacking in the latter. She hurries along between them for one minute and fifteen seconds exactly before she halts again, and listens.

The steps are still coming, and they are getting closer. Somehow, her pursuers can determine which way she moves through this labyrinth of passages, which suggests that attempting to conceal herself and her robots in a chamber is foolish: there is little chance the Red Corsairs will run heedlessly past. Are her movements simply too predictable? Or is there a surveillance system of which she is not aware? Is the ship itself communing with its masters in some way? Griza would have dismissed such a notion as fanciful not too long ago, but she has seen the silently screaming faces in the walls, and she knows that the machine-spirit of the *Spectre of Ruin* is foul and corrupted. It is far from impossible that the renegades are being guided unerringly after her by the very thing in which she is attempting to hide.

Still, she has not been caught yet. If stealth will not work, then speed will have to suffice. Her automata will have power to move for hours, if not days, and she herself is relatively tireless, thanks to the myriad bionics that now make up a large part of her body. Space Marines possess unnatural endurance as well, of course, but with any luck they will be called away to other duties before they can catch her, or perhaps will abandon the pursuit in search of easier prey. Even if she is caught, she will not go down without a fight.

As she sets off again, she considers the ramifications of fighting a pitched battle against Red Corsairs Space Marines in the bowels of Huron Blackheart's flagship. The Blood Reaver will not tolerate such defiance on her part, she is sure, no matter what claims he has made of might making right. That will seal her doom – but if the choice is between certain doom now, or apparently certain doom in the future, Griza will take the second option. Dying tomorrow may be a permanent risk, but it is better than dying today.

Either she has not been paying proper attention to the admittedly incomplete schematics she has formatted for the *Spectre*, or she has stumbled into an area for which she has no data, or the ship itself has twisted its nature: whichever the truth is, she and her escort emerge from the narrow corridor down which they have been hurrying and step onto a wide platform. It is bordered with safety rails that were once sturdy and which are now corroded, and it narrows to a ten-foot-wide walkway that spans a chasm Griza estimates at at least one hundred yards across, and with a depth that she cannot easily calculate.

More pressingly, there are six Red Corsairs around her, each with their bolters raised.

She does not have time to properly update her kastelans' programming. With the correct protocols in place, they would be more than a match even for these half-dozen heretics. Without them, her automata will operate on a very basic self-preservation programme that will likely see them overwhelmed and destroyed, and her with them.

'Hold your fire!' one of the renegades shouts. He is a brute of a warrior, who appears to have swollen inside and in some places through his armour, and now possesses skin the colour of blood and completely white, featureless eyes. It is not immediately clear to Griza whether he is addressing her or his companions, but although she has her gamma pistol ready and concealed in the sleeve of her robe, she does not aim it at him.

'Datasmith,' the same warrior says, with a smile that may have been intended as ingratiating, and if so utterly fails. 'Lord Huron commands your presence.'

TEN

The *Macragge's Honour* translates again after just over seven hours, at least as time is experienced on the *Spectre of Ruin*, and Huron barks the order to follow them. The ship's warp engines provide one final pulse of power, and they slide out of the raging torrents of the empyrean into another crossover zone, where the tides of the warp run weaker and mingle with realspace. They are still in the Maelstrom – Huron can feel that in his bones – but not anywhere he has been before.

That is not surprising. Even the Master of the Maelstrom knows only a fraction of the area over which he claims dominion, and the very nature of the tortured space within it means that things can change without warning.

'Tactical,' Huron rasps, taking a deep breath. There is a bone-deep weariness within him that is quite different from the banked fires of pain that are his ever-present companions, or the sharp muscle ache that can afflict even an Astartes warrior should they have been subjected to tremendous exertion over a sustained period of time. This is a psychic fatigue, for Huron has spent a great deal of effort in keeping track of the *Macragge's Honour* under challenging circumstances. His thoughts feel slow and laboured, and he is ruefully aware that if Verngar has predicted his actions well enough to draw the *Spectre of Ruin* into an ambush, in an attempt to stage a coup, Huron may find himself lacking the sharpness of mind he will need to ensure victory.

'No other vessels except the *Macragge's Honour*, lord,' the Master of Auspex says shakily. It had been a rough translation for the humans, for all that it had been a partial one, and the acrid smell of vomit adds a new layer to the already foetid air of the ship's bridge. 'We've emerged from the warp not far from a planet.'

'Show me,' Huron commands. The fizzing and humming of machinery rises in volume, as instruments that had been faced with the confusing, blinding immaterium now begin to process their surroundings properly once more.

'Hail from the *Macragge's Honour*,' comes the call, and Huron grins like a deep-sea predator.

'Let's hear it.'

'Lord Huron. This is an unexpected honour.'

'Unexpected', was it? So Verngar was going to pretend he had not noticed the *Spectre of Ruin* shadowing his ship through the warp, and that he had not been trying to lose them. Very well.

'If what you say about the power of this artefact is true, I would like to be present for its recovery,' Huron says. 'Besides, we both know how deceitful any servant of Tzeentch can be, let alone Kairos Fateweaver. I would hate to see so competent a commander of mine fall valiantly while fighting off a trap that had been laid for him, when the presence of another ship could have turned the tide.'

'Had I known you were following, I could have ensured that we communicated our changes of heading,' Verngar says. *'We could have coordinated our strategy.'*

There is a hint of rebuke in the Apostate's voice: not enough to be a challenge, not yet, but enough to communicate to any who hear it that Huron's course of action might not have been the wisest. Yes, Verngar is starting to test the boundaries of his overlord's authority. An easy thing to do while sitting in a phenomenally powerful battleship which, while it might not recognise him as its commander, will certainly see Huron and the *Spectre of Ruin* as an enemy.

'Had someone on your ship known I was following, such a trap might have been altered or abandoned,' Huron replies smoothly. 'Unless you have complete confidence in all of your underlings, Verngar?'

It is a ridiculous question. No follower of the Ruinous Powers can boast such a thing, and Huron's statement is in itself a veiled barb to remind Verngar that his actions are not going unnoticed. For a moment, Huron feels a pang of loss for the days when all those who wore his colours admired and respected him; when he was seen as their rightful leader, instead of a tyrant whose presence was to be tolerated only until sufficient power could be found to usurp him.

He shunts the thoughts away. Such loyalties were built on the lies of the Imperium and its moribund structures, and he has no use for them. He keeps his position now through power and ingenuity, not the mindless obedience of others. If he cannot fight off challengers to his throne, what right does he have to occupy it?

'Where have you brought us, Verngar?' he asks, when the

Apostate does not reply to his question. He turns his attention to the read-outs, seeking to garner what information he can without Verngar's input.

'The world is known as Kyren,' Verngar replies. *'The Changer's influence lies strongly over it.'*

That much is true, from what Huron can see. The hololith images, being translucent, are not the best at depicting the textures of a planet, but Kyren's deep purples and reds look almost glossy. Huron's gaze flickers over read-out after read-out, assessing the information in microseconds, then re-evaluating conclusions as updates appear.

'High silicate readings,' he muses. '*Very* high… Verngar, the planet appears to be made primarily of glass.'

'Indeed so, Lord Huron.'

Huron snorts, and checks the atmospheric data. 'The air appears moderately tolerable for mortals. Although…' He eyes a sudden spike in sulphur readings. 'Changeable. As might be expected.'

'It should cause us no concerns, given that the planet has a sizeable population. The population itself might prove a hindrance to our efforts, however.'

There are life signs, many of them. Kyren's position within this area of reality-warping space means that it is hard for mundane instruments to get a completely accurate picture, but the *Spectre*'s sensors are telling Huron that there is little in the way of industry, or other indications of what the Imperium would consider civilisation. Instead, the bulk of inhabitants appear to be living a primitive existence, which is only to be expected on such an outlandish world.

For a moment, Huron ponders how such numbers of mortal creatures have survived here, given the hostile nature of the planet, but he dismisses the thought. Such questions are pointless in regard to a world over which Tzeentch holds sway, where natural rules will have been bent at the very least, if not broken entirely.

'I am assuming you have a more specific understanding of the Ebon Talon's location than simply "this planet"?' he enquires.

'Yes, lord. There is a large mountain shaped somewhat like a clawed hand that stands alone near the eastern coast of the largest northern continent. My rituals have ascertained that the relic should reside there.'

Huron manipulates the image in front of him to bring up the landmark Verngar has described. He frowns, and overlays onto the hololith the information regarding life signs.

'The area around the mountain appears to be one of the most densely populated areas.'

'Indeed, Lord Huron. I suspect the artefact is the object of considerable reverence for the creatures that dwell here. It is highly likely that they regularly war over possession of this site.'

Huron grunts. 'Let me ensure I am clear in your meaning. You propose that we land on this planet in the middle of what could well be an unending holy war, and take from them the artefact over which they so zealously fight?'

'That is correct.'

Huron smiles. 'I knew there was a reason I raised you to a position of command, Verngar. I will link up with you and your forces on the surface.' He signals to the vox-officer, who cuts the link.

'Should I contact the teleportarium, lord?' Tagron asks. The huscarl's voice is eager; clearly the slaughter of the tarellians only whetted his appetite for combat.

'No, old friend,' Huron replies. 'We have insufficient information on the geography, the likely resistance or the exact location of this artefact. If the Apostate speaks true then it will likely be in a shrine of some sort, but such a place will be almost impossible to locate from orbit. We will deploy our forces close to the target and fight our way in overland. We will insert on *Bloodstrike*.'

He smiles again.

'And someone go and find me Magos Dallax. I feel like seeing what her vaunted automata can do in battle, and I would not want her to miss this experience.'

ELEVEN

Kastelan combat automata were never designed to fit into a Stormbird gunship, but Huron insisted, and Griza Dallax has clearly already learned her place sufficiently not to argue. So it is that the datasmith's maniple of cybernetic war machines has taken up uneasy station in the passenger hold, opposite Huron and his five huscarls, and the nine members of the squad who call themselves The Scourging. Their leader is the former Black Legionnaire Huron saw earlier, who salutes him with a fist thumped into his breastplate. Despite abandoning his old allegiance, he sports a high topknot not dissimilar to that worn by the Warmaster. Huron eyes him.

'You're not an original Cthonian, are you?' he observes.

'No, Lord Huron,' the Space Marine replies thickly. His tongue is too large for his mouth, his flesh is slightly scaled, and the tips of two tusks are just beginning to protrude from the end of his jaw. 'I was forged for the first assault on Terra.'

Ten thousand years old, Huron muses with grim humour, and this warrior's command consists solely of another eight of his own kind. Huron has lived for over four hundred years, but even his enhanced mind can barely comprehend the thought of a hundred centuries. Still, he is reasonably certain that had he lived for so long and achieved so little, he would have surrendered to despair.

Then again, for all the fact that the First Legions are so proud about turning on the stifling mindsets of the early Imperium, many of the individuals still think in no more complicated terms than battle and killing. For those who have given themselves over to Khorne, that is practically all they can ever think of.

'What is your name?' Huron asks. A warrior who believes his commander takes an interest in him will fight harder, in order to impress.

'Yariel, lord.'

'Heed me well, Yariel,' Huron says. He does not need to raise his voice to ensure his words reach the rest of the squad; their enhanced hearing will suffice. 'The Apostate must not reach what we seek before me.'

'Will you be leaving your guards behind then, lord?' one of Yariel's squad asks, with a rough laugh. Tagron growls in response, and the tension in the Stormbird rises a little, but the warrior is not without a point: the ancient Terminator suits of Huron's huscarls are marvels of ancient engineering that can withstand all but the heaviest gunfire and turn even the keenest blade, but they are ponderous and slow.

However, Huron is not much quicker himself, these days.

'I will not, because I have no need to make compromises,' he says calmly. 'I have stated my expectations – see that you live up to them.' The warrior who spoke is helmed, so Huron cannot see his face, but his body language subsides a little. Insubordination might be a more frequent occurrence within the renegade legions than it is in their Imperial counterparts, but the punishments for it can be considerably more capricious and severe.

'Ready to launch, master,' Carazzalan says into his ear. Huron trudges to the rack and secures himself.

'Then do so.'

Bloodstrike's engines fire up with a whine that rises to a roar, and it takes off from the deck of the *Spectre of Ruin*'s hangar bay, then kicks out into the darkness beyond. It rolls to starboard, bringing the richly coloured orb of Kyren into view, and plunges towards the planet.

Huron looks over at where Magos Dallax is strapped in, between the hulking figures of her kastelans, who are mag-clamped to the deck. The datasmith lacks the bulk of a Space Marine, but has still ensured that she is in no danger of being thrown around by the gunship's manoeuvres. Huron detects no sign of fear or nausea in her, but that is not surprising: the servants of the Machine-God rarely retain their biological methods of balance, and he suspects she has become quite accustomed to the presence of threat over the last few days.

'How have you found the hospitality of my ship, magos?' he asks. Her hood comes up and the visual sensors within meet his gaze.

'I and my charges remain fully functional. Lord.'

Huron finds this response a little disappointing in its lack of detail – he had hoped for some tale of her terror – but if she is telling the truth then at least she and her automata should perform adequately in the field. It is possible, of course, that she could order them to attack him now; in this enclosed space, even he might not survive such an assassination attempt.

However, that would surely doom her, in this ancient craft plunging towards a warp-twisted world, and Huron does not think Griza Dallax is ready to abandon her continued existence just yet.

He opens a vox-channel back to the *Spectre of Ruin*. 'Commence bombard-ment.'

'Acknowledged, Lord Huron.'

That gets the magos' attention. Her lenses click and whirr as she focuses on him more fully. 'You intend your ship to fire on the planet while we are between its guns and the surface, Lord Huron?'

'Do I hear the echo of incredulity in your voice, magos?' Huron chuckles. 'Fear not. Traitors and heretics we may be, in the eyes of those who worship the Corpse-Emperor, but we still make war with the precision of our deluded kin. Observe.'

Brilliant flashes of light illuminate the Stormbird's interior as the space between the *Spectre of Ruin* and Kyren's surface is lit up by the strobing of war. Mighty macrocannon shells tear silently past at supersonic speeds before thundering into the atmosphere beneath, while pulses of turbolaser batteries briefly link warship and ground. More distant flashes of light are visible now, as the *Macragge's Honour* opens fire in its turn, to take the northern half of the rough circle that Huron has traced out.

'What is the purpose of this?' Dallax dares to ask. 'I understood that you were seeking to recover a relic, not destroy one.'

'The mountain in which the item rests is at the centre of a great conflict,' Huron informs her. 'My warriors can cut through the chaff that will stand in our way, but even the keenest blades can be weighed down by weight of numbers. We are not firing on the mountain – we are ringing it with death so that reinforcements cannot fall on us from behind as we cleave our way towards our goal.' The Red Corsairs will isolate the enemy, cut through them, take what they want, and leave: it is a method of attack that has served him well time and time again over the last century.

Dallax hesitates for a moment before speaking again. 'How wide is this ring?'

'Fifteen miles from edge to edge, with a kill-zone approximately one mile wide,' Huron replies.

'And the estimated density of the enemies in that area?'

'At least ten thousand per square mile,' Huron says lazily.

When the magos speaks again, her mechanical voice somehow manages to communicate both fear and awe. 'You would take nearly *half a million lives* simply to gain this artefact?'

Huron laughs with genuine amusement. 'I took more lives for less cause when I still served the Imperium! And I would take far more, if I had need to. The path of my success is paved with the bodies of the dead, magos! I would kill every living thing on the planet, if it would benefit me.'

Something stirs within him as he speaks those words; the urge to enact them, to slaughter an entire world in the name of his own glory. He fights it down. He knows from where such urges come, and it is not his own glory: he has no wish to stray into servitude to the Brass Throne.

'As it is,' he continues, 'to do so would be an expenditure of time and resources that may well outweigh the gains I can achieve here. In any case, you should not concern yourself,' he adds. 'The lives down there are twisted by the Ruinous Powers, yet do not serve me. Whether your loyalties lie with the Red Corsairs, or still with your former masters, they should be nothing to you except vermin to be exterminated.'

'Yes,' Dallax says after a moment, with a jerk of her cowled head in passable imitation of a normal human's nod. 'Yes, of course. They should be... exterminated. Lord.'

'A combat drop just isn't the same without anti-aircraft fire,' one of Yariel's squad comments. 'You don't feel as alive.' He carries an ancient plasma gun, and at some point his left arm has been replaced by a metal bionic. Regardless of its original provenance, the prosthetic is now as pitted and stained as the rest of its owner's armour plate, is crusted with old blood, and has flaws in the visible metal that look just a little like screaming faces. Huron notices that Dallax's optics keep flicking momentarily towards it.

'I can shoot you if you want, Tarmogren,' Yariel replies, unholstering his bolt pistol. The chuckles that run through the rest of the squad tell Huron that this is within the realms of normal conversation for these warriors as they prepare to enter combat, and there is not actually about to be a gunfight breaking out in the belly of *Bloodstrike*. Griza Dallax seems less certain of herself, judging by the way her fingers are creeping towards the nearest of her automata, as though to goad them into protective action.

'Have you ever seen war, magos?' Huron asks her, before she starts the very fight she apparently fears.

'My maniple and I have participated in fourteen separate combat situations in service to the Omnissiah,' Dallax responds instantly, then abruptly falls silent as she realises that she has named her god in front of a gunship full of heretics.

'I didn't ask if you'd seen combat,' Huron says, his voice grating out through his smile. 'I asked if you'd seen *war*.'

'I do not comprehend the distinction to which you appear to be referring. Lord.'

'Combat is a fight,' Huron tells her. 'It can be a quick action, a matter of survival or acquisition. *Combat* is ten warriors falling on one enemy and overwhelming him. *Combat* is a sniper taking a shot from a mile away and executing a commander, without ever being in danger of reprisal. *War* is the real thing.

'War is where no inch of the ground has been left free of the impact of boot or track or bomb. War is where the air is smoke that hides the face of a sun too afraid to see what has transpired below it. War is where the question is not *if* there have been casualties, but how many – it is where your heartbeat is the thunder of the guns and your war cry is the scream of shells, and your blood is separated from that of others only by the thickness of your skin.'

Yariel's squad have forgotten their bickering, and are rapt in attention. Even Huron's huscarls are listening.

'No, lord,' Dallax replies. 'No, I have not.'

'War is what we were made for,' Huron says softly. 'That is a truth far deeper and more primal than anything your clockwork Emperor has ever cogitated. The Imperium called us the Angels of Death, and they thought to place us on a leash like a biddable pet – merely the latest folly in a list of arrogances that spreads back to before the Great Crusade!'

He draws his power axe and thumbs the activation rune, lighting up the blade with the crackling field that will lend it an edge more fierce than anything that could be created by physical matter alone.

'Be ready, little datasmith. Do not fall behind.'

'I assure you, lord, my automata are more than capable of keeping up,' Dallax says stiffly.

Huron grins at her. He realises that it is absurd for him to be proud of having stung her pride – he, who has just unleashed destruction on the planet below! – but mass murder should not distract one from the little cruelties of life.

Besides, a datasmith who feels her charges have been slighted might be motivated to prove him wrong, which under the circumstances is likely to only work in his favour.

'War is about more than just the ability to move swiftly,' he tells her. 'It is about knowing when to move, where to move, where and how to fight. Your robots are faster, stronger and more durable than any of my warriors, and yet without a mind to guide them they are nearly useless. You must understand war, datasmith, or you and your kastelans will perish on this warp-tainted world.'

'That will not happen,' Dallax says defiantly.

'Good,' Huron replies, as *Bloodstrike* begins to pull up from its dive. Normally it would be jinking and swerving as it flies into a contested landing zone, but as Tarmogren observed, there are no dangers to it here. Huron hears the chatter of the hull-mounted weapons as it slows, and then begins to swing in a slow circle to clear a place to touch down. All around them, he knows, other transports will be performing similar actions. At any moment, the first drop pods should land. Everything has been timed with an exactness that would have made any official of the Adeptus Administratum proud, had it not been executed by beings that would have caused said official to soil themselves in terror.

Bloodstrike lands, settling onto landing gear that is millennia old, and the ramp under the nose lowers. Sound crashes in: the boom of explosives, the roar of bolters, the chatter of high-velocity weaponry, and screams of the injured and dying so numerous as to form a chorus.

Huron takes a breath. He can smell the exhaust fumes of Stormbirds and Thunderhawks, the acrid tang of bolter propellant and the faintly sulphurous air of the planet itself. He unfastens the straps holding him in place, and his warriors do the same. He raises the Tyrant's Claw and points to the eerie, flickering light of the exterior, where a landscape of twisted glass is illuminated by the tortured skies above.

'To war!'

TWELVE

Kyren is at once vastly different from any other world on which Huron Blackheart has made war, and yet the same.

The surface underfoot is not mud, or grass, or even rock: it is glass, glass that has been twisted and sculpted by whatever passes for natural processes and weathering here. The ground rises and falls in crests and hollows, but the crests are jagged and sharp, and the hollows are filled with dust that glitters gently when the light from above washes over it; for the dust too is glass, just ground down into powder. The surface beneath Huron's feet contains rich veins of purple and turquoise, but the ridges fade into colourlessness as they rise, suggesting that the source of the pigment is buried somewhere deep down. The sky above contains no sun or even stars, and is composed of a shifting, shimmering aurora that melts in and out of shapes which are nearly recognisable, but morph into something else before the mind can truly identify them.

Other things, however, are more familiar. The wind that gusts around them and causes Yariel's topknot to whip like it is a living thing also carries the thunder of guns, and the smell of blood. The mountain that rises in front of him is like nothing he has seen before – the summit is not just shaped a little like a claw, it is as though a god has sculpted the glass of this world into a massive representation of a clawed hand, which is quite possibly what has actually happened – but it is still just a target. They have landed on the lower slopes, and Huron can see the paths that wind up its sides.

He has no more time to assess the situation before the enemy arrives, charging between drop-ships and drop pods, and throwing themselves at the troops disembarking from them.

They are broadly human, or at least once came from human stock. Some are swollen with musculature to near-Astartes proportions, others are tall and unnaturally spindle-thin, some are squat, some are massively fat, and many are no more unremarkable in terms of their build than Huron's human troops. Their physical characteristics are as varied, too: horns or fangs, fingernails that have become talons and hands that have turned into crustacean-like pincers, or stabbing blades of bone, or crushing maces of scarred gristle. Some have a tail; some have two. Some have fur, or scales, or skin of no shade that occurs naturally within human biology. Some have extra arms; a few have an additional head. One mighty slab of flesh has no head at all, but eyes and a leering mouth set into its bare chest. Here and there, Huron sees a firearm – a shotgun, a battered autopistol, a primitive blunderbuss or jezail – but in the main, the attackers make do with melee weapons, whether that be blades and clubs, or the tools of their own twisted bodies.

They die, of course, and quickly. Even Huron's poorest

troops, the unaugmented humans that make up the rabble of his force, are better equipped than these wretches. Most of them have little fear of such mutations, either: in fact many sport their own, and so there is no hesitation of shock or disgust such as might be the case if an Astra Militarum regiment were suddenly faced by such a deformed enemy. Guns chatter into life and blood sprays, and the attackers begin to fall. Some close the distance and their weapons begin to bite, but the Red Corsairs have no use for cowards or incompetents: the humans under Huron's command fight back with knives, flails and bludgeons.

Where the new arrivals encounter Space Marines, the combat is considerably less even.

'Cut them down!' Huron roars, stepping forwards. The Scourging lets loose with a volley of bolter shells that turns an on-rushing mob of mutants into mangled flesh and a mist of blood as efficiently as any sorcerous incantation, but Huron shoulders his way through them and grabs Yariel by his pauldron with the Tyrant's Claw. He does not activate the power field, but the strength of his grip by itself is enough to dent his underling's armour.

'Save your ammunition!' Huron rasps. He gestures around them. The warring factions have thrown themselves against the newcomers with just as much fury as they employ against each other, and they are everywhere. 'We may need it for sterner opposition than this! Shoot sparingly – otherwise, it's knife work.'

'Aye, lord,' Yariel growls in response. He holsters his bolt pistol, and takes his long, antiquated chainsword in a two-handed grip. 'You heard the Blood Reaver! Time to redden our hands!'

They surge forwards, towards the mountain. The glass under

their feet makes for tricky progress, for although its surface is far from smooth, it still provides momentary losses of friction sufficient for even a Space Marine to slip on occasion. Kyren's warriors seem to be familiar with this treacherous aspect of their planet, for while they too lose their footing from time to time, they are nowhere near as clumsy as Huron might have expected. Half a dozen appear above, massing on the edge of a ridge and clearly preparing to hurl themselves down at the warriors below. Huron raises the Tyrant's Claw and briefly bathes them in burning promethium, and they fall back, screaming and slapping at the flames that stick stubbornly to their clothes and flesh. The ground on which they were standing begins to crack and shatter as the heat takes its toll, and the edges of it start to crumble down in a fine drizzle of dust that sparkles in the reflected aurora lights from above.

It occurs to Huron what a beautiful thing it would be to destroy a planet such as this one: to see it blasted apart not into ugly chunks of rock and rapidly cooling magma, but multifaceted shards of glass that will reflect both each other and the glory of the twisted space of the warp as they tumble over and around and away from each other. It would be an ever-expanding flower of destruction, and he would be the artist.

He stamps down on the thought, even as Yariel's chainsword takes an onrushing attacker in the neck. To give himself over to such an excess of destruction in the pursuit of aesthetic pleasure would be to allow the Dark Prince a clawhold on his soul, and Huron has no time for such things. The Ruinous Powers continue to set their snares for his spirit, casting their lures and weaving temptations that seek to amplify his own desires until he is in thrall to them.

'No, I don't think so,' Huron growls to himself. He ignores

the look one of Yariel's squad gives him at hearing the Blood Reaver utter such a non sequitur.

The ground is starting to rise properly now, and they will have to pick a route up the side of the mountain. Huron assesses their options: several paths wind up there, and each one is clogged by those who were already fighting over the possession of this place before he even arrived. Other than that, no one route appears to offer a notably easier option than the rest.

'Take the closest,' he orders, checking around them to try to gain a wider tactical appraisal of the situation. Not all of his forces are converging on the mountain; that would lead to a choke point just as bad as anything already occurring. The majority are spreading out to engage and delay anyone who would seek to prevent him from reaching his goal.

He cannot make Verngar out, which is causing him some concern. There are dark red knots of Astartes pushing forward, but Huron can see none that carry the personal banner of the Apostate, the bat-winged crossed swords burned onto the stretched-out skin of an Imperial Fists Codicier. It is almost certainly too much to hope for that Verngar's landing craft was swatted from the sky by an errant macrocannon shell.

He could reach out, of course, and send his consciousness racing across this battlefield in an attempt to locate his ambitious commander. However, while such an action is less threatening to his psyche than when surrounded by the currents of the warp, it is also more difficult, and he can still feel the hollowness in his bones from the exertions that guided them here. He will need to be as alert as possible, so deadening his mind by trying to find the Apostate is a luxury he will not allow himself yet.

Otherworldly screams ring out, and Huron looks up. Half a

dozen avian shapes soar overhead: his Raptors, borne aloft by the screeching, fume-belching power of their jump packs. They swoop down, aiming beyond the next ridge, presumably to plunge into a knot of warriors they have spied from on high.

They never get there.

A crackling nimbus of energy surrounds them, and the Raptors' voices shift from the hunting cries of predators to shrill shrieks of pain and panic. They hang in mid-air for a moment, the jets of their jump packs straining against the unseen power which holds them in place. Then the tendrils of power thicken, and darken, and the corrupted Space Marines begin to crumple in on themselves. Huron hears a gasp of astonishment and horror from Griza Dallax as the Raptors are crushed inwards, screaming as they go, until each one is nothing more than a dark red lump. These spiral together and fuse under the immense pressure being exerted on them, before dropping heavily to the ground as a chunk of compressed ceramite and flesh no larger than a Mark VII helmet. The entire process has taken under five seconds.

The culprit is not hard to determine. It would make sense that a planet under the aegis of the Changer of Ways would boast more than its fair share of sorcerers.

The warriors who had been the Raptors' targets come over and around the next ridge, bellowing war cries as they do so. Huron counts at least fifty of them, but he has eyes only for the shape that walks in their midst.

The sorceress is tall, a head taller than most of her cohort, and carries a metal staff topped with a shaped chunk of the planet itself. Her skin is the palest blue, and her eyes burn with literal flames that lick up over her brow, yet inflict no visible damage. Her head puts forth no hair, only long, dark purple feathered plumes that shake and sway in the wind. She focuses on Huron and raises one surprisingly normal-looking hand towards him, her fingers crooked into a claw shape.

The Hamadrya chitters, and Huron's world darkens and slows.

He can see the lines of force, can read the tendrils of the warp as the sorceress draws power in from her twisted surroundings, from the energy that lies at the core of this strange world and from the shimmering heavens above. He sees her mouth shape whatever incantation she uses to mould the power to her will, watches the slight spread of her fingers as she releases it: a needless conceit, but the self-taught so often associate a physical gesture with what is a purely mental exercise.

Huron does not know exactly how, but he can also see the paths along which he must guide his own will to sever the spell's power, and he does so without any further thought. The sorceress staggers as she feels her attack not just blunted or resisted, but stolen from her entirely, and those burning eyes widen in shock. Now the destructive energy coils invisibly around Huron's hands, for him to do with as he pleases.

Around him, massive shapes surge forward and begin to pulverise the sorceress' warriors. The combat maniple of Griza Dallax does not bother with their destructive heavy phosphor blasters, but simply smash the mutants to death with their enormous fists. Yariel's squad and Huron's huscarls hang back and watch with a mixture of amusement and awe as the automata bludgeon their way to victory in a matter of seconds, earning new bloodstains over the ones the datasmith had deliberately placed on their armoured shells.

Huron concentrates, and the power he stole from the sorceress whips back towards her, binding her with the same tendrils of energy she used to crush the Raptors. The staff falls from her hands and she drops to her knees with a gasp of pain and anger. He walks forward to loom over her, even as the last of her followers are brained by a kastelan.

'You have power, and will,' Huron rasps. 'There is a place for you in my ranks, if you wish it.'

She stares up at him, her expression carved into one of hatred. 'I am no man's slave.'

The sorceress' voice is low and smooth, and puts Huron fleetingly in mind of a cultured Imperial diplomat he knew once, from the days before he was betrayed. He nods in acknowledgement, a gesture of respect.

'An attitude with which I can identify. As you wish.' He releases the spell to fulfil its original purpose, and the sorceress is crushed within instants by the very energies she herself originally summoned. The stolen power drains away from Huron, and leaves him feeling slightly empty.

He could find more, of course. He was never a psyker, but the gifts he received after he made his bargains have opened up new insights and abilities to him. Here, on this planet, it would be an easy matter for him to plunge more deeply into his connection to the warp through the Hamadrya and increase his understanding. He could siphon off the power of the world, and that which drips down so plentifully from the skies above, and bend what passes for reality here to his will. He need only reach out his hand and call, and the Ebon Talon will be summoned to him…

And Tzeentch will have a hold over him. Huron spits onto a nearby corpse in disgust. He long ago wearied of the games of the Dark Gods, but he has no choice other than to play them, and be eternally on his guard against their blandishments. He knew that before he ever made his deals with them, and he is not the type to whine about the consequences of his own decisions.

Griza Dallax is staring at the crushed remains of the sorceress. Huron wonders if she is comparing the defiance of this Chaos worshipper to her own self-preservation, and finding herself wanting.

'Move on!' he snarls, jolting his warriors into action once more. 'I'll not let the Apostate claim this prize!'

THIRTEEN

The mountain paths are narrow and treacherous, and the slick footing is ever more deadly. Now a slip does not just mean a moment of inconvenience, or even an opening in which an opponent might strike: now it can mean a lethal plunge against which even ceramite plating offers no protection.

One of The Scourging is killed by a slug from a black-powder jezail, of all things. Being struck in the chest by such a projectile would be beneath his notice under normal circumstances, but the almost imperceptible shift it causes in his balance makes his weight move just far enough for his foot to lose its grip, and then he is toppling. Guarding against too-quick movements of their own, none of his squad reacts in time, and he disappears from sight over the edge. The vox fills with his curses for a few moments – curses against the warrior who shot him, curses against his fellows for not saving him, curses against the Emperor as a matter of general principle – and then there is only static.

Huron reaches out past the Terminator-armoured form of Frakn and triggers the heavy flamer of the Tyrant's Claw. The flames roar out, and in such narrow conditions the victims have no chance of avoiding them. They scream, and they burn, and they fall in their turn.

And beneath their feet, the glass of the path cracks.

'Perhaps, lord,' Frakn suggests, 'you might refrain from deploying your weapon, for now.'

Huron chuckles wryly at his huscarl's words. 'A wise suggestion. Very well. I will leave the killing to others, until we reach firmer footing.'

They advance cautiously, but although the path is now crazed with cracks, it holds even for Dallax's kastelans. They have now climbed higher than most of the rest of the combatants, having fought their way through the various factions seeking to gain control of the mountain, and Huron can see the battle playing out far below as the rest of his forces hold back the rest.

Or at least, they should be. He can make out only the broadest outlines from up here, but a knot of what must be his own cultists, who had been maintaining their position, have turned on the warriors next to them in the Red Corsairs' rough defensive line. He recalls the planned deployment and activates his vox.

'What's happening down there?' he demands. 'Aumaxon, report.'

'The mortals have been twisted by the planet, lord,' Aumaxon Dykarr replies. If he is surprised at being hailed by his master from atop a mountain, his voice gives no indication of it. Huron hears the roar of his combi-bolter, and then the sharp, rising hiss as he fires the melta component. *'The wind carried dust thrown up by the bombardment over us not long ago, and they*

must have breathed it in. Their flesh is weak, and began to turn – it seems their minds have followed.'

Huron growls in disgust. 'Ensure our brethren have their helmets affixed. I'll not lose any of our own to this place.'

'As you say, Lord Huron.'

Huron himself wears no helmet, for the surgeries have left his skull misshapen, and virtually incompatible with such a device. Besides, he prefers to let his enemies see the ruin of his face; he is not ashamed by it, and he wants them to know without question who it is that is killing them. His lungs are more than capable of handling any of the usual contaminants that his helmet would filter out, and as for mutagenic dust, he believes that it will take more than that to twist his body out of his control.

He may be right, he may be wrong, but he will never again hide his face behind ceramite. If he is to die, he will die with the wind on his skin.

Yariel's squad pushes forwards, using a slightly wider area of path to slip by Huron and his slower huscarls, and scout ahead around the mountain's next spur. Dallax's automata are bringing up the rear, ready to fight off anyone attempting to fall on them from behind. So far the datasmith has acted as Huron would have expected: deploying her robots to formidable effect if she feels threatened, or if he has expressly commanded it, but otherwise letting the Space Marines handle the bulk of the combat.

Huron does not mind. It is amusing to gradually break her spirit by leading her along and making her think she is choosing her own actions. She no longer has to think before calling him 'lord'. Soon she will realise that her continued survival will be best assured by serving his interests, and then he will have her completely. Whatever will remain of her independence will be buried deep – perhaps not deep enough that she forgets it, or even realises that it is no longer a factor in her thinking, but certainly enough that it will not guide her.

Besides, the kastelans have barely used any power or ammunition, which means they could prove to be the telling factor if things get desperate. For all their caution, the rest of Huron's entourage are beginning to run low on bolter shells, and Frakn's reaper autocannon has perhaps three good bursts left. Huron would reflect on the difficulties of waging war without the support of the Imperium's supply lines, were he not all too aware of the regular failings of the Adeptus Administratum.

'Lord Huron!' Yariel's voice growls into his ear. *'We have reached a cave, which looks to be an entrance into the mountain's interior!'*

'Excellent,' Huron replies, trudging onwards. 'Secure it. We will be with you momentarily.'

'It is good that you are here, my lord.'

That voice, broadcast over the general vox, does not belong to Yariel. Huron recognises Verngar's tones, and suppresses a snarl of irritation. The Apostate will still have his uses, but only so long as he does not claim the Ebon Talon and raise his standing too far in the eyes of the other Red Corsairs. Huron can use even an ambitious commander that still knows his place – an ambitious one with knives bared cannot be tolerated.

'I'm glad to see you've managed to keep up, Verngar,' he replies, to snorts of laughter from his huscarls. Huron's slower pace is well known, if not openly commented on by those who wish to retain the use of their own legs.

'There is no power that could prevent me from being here, my lord,' Verngar rumbles. *'We are closing in on our destiny.'*

Huron notes the eagerness in the Apostate's voice. It is not the voice of a warrior striving for the glory of his warlord, or his legion. It is the voice of an egomaniacal fanatic.

Huron might accept that he could also be labelled as egomaniacal, but he is assuredly not a fanatic. Fanatics are blinkered, and their obsessions miss the big picture; either that or their picture is so wide and all-encompassing that they have no time for the details. It is one reason why he has so little time for the Word Bearers. By the time they finish their prayers, rituals and sacrifices, the Red Corsairs could have already killed half of whatever enemy was arrayed against them.

He rounds the bend in the path and sees the cave entrance, which sits in a glass wall that leads up to eventually fold over and become the clawed hand of the mountain's peak. The cave itself is at least twenty feet high and three times that across, with jagged crystals – jutting up from the floor and down from the ceiling just inside the mouth – that bear more than a passing resemblance to giant, glossy fangs. Liquid flows from between the lower outcrops, spilling across the ledge in front of the cave before tumbling over the edge to turn into a waterfall that plunges in an unbroken sheet for at least two hundred feet before finally surrendering to the power of the wind and being blown away into a spray.

At least, it would be a waterfall, if the liquid were water. But it is not.

'Is that... blood?' Magos Dallax asks, with more hesitation than Huron would have expected from one of the Adeptus Mechanicus. Still, it is more likely that her mind is rebelling against the presence of a constant flow of this much blood in this location, rather than any sort of more visceral reaction to its nature.

Huron inhales, and detects the tang of salt and copper. 'It

is. Human blood. Remarkably untainted by mutation, as well, given the condition of the life here.'

'But how is this possible?' Dallax demands. Huron can imagine the logic-engines that will have undoubtedly replaced portions of her brain frantically running calculations and scenarios, as they try to comprehend what her optical sensors are witnessing.

'You're in the Maelstrom, magos,' he tells her. 'That is all the answer you need.' He strides forward, just as more shapes in dark red armour appear on the far side of the entrance.

There is Verngar the Apostate, flanked on one side by Turazan the Warpsmith, and on the other by a sorcerer – not Garlon Souleater, or any from Huron's main cabal, but Huron can read the sigils carved into the warrior's armour, and taste the warp energy that clings to him. An outsider, then: one who is excluded from the higher echelons of power that the sorcerers have built within the ranks of the Red Corsairs, and likely looking for advancement as much as Verngar is. Ambitious, but probably not so closely leashed to Verngar that he will not abandon him if the Apostate's star begins to dim. A double-edged sword in truth, and one that Huron might be able to wield, or which might turn in his hand and cut him.

Behind Verngar comes his honour guard: close on twenty Red Corsairs, variously armed with bolters, bolt pistols and chainswords. The two factions are relatively even in terms of numbers, but should it come to combat – which is a possibility that Huron always, *always* considers – it could play out extremely lopsidedly.

Verngar is a fearsome fighter, especially when in the grip of his blood rage. Huron believes that he has the beating of the Apostate, should it come to it, but Huron is also the only member of his party who has any real chance of neutralising the sorcerer. Turazan is deadly in a number of ways, and cannot be underestimated, should he decide to throw in his lot against his lord. The Red Corsairs that accompany Verngar would struggle to make an impact against Huron's huscarls and Dallax's kastelans, but that assumes that Dallax would commit herself to such a fight, and also that Turazan is not able to incapacitate the Imperial robots using Mechanicum tricks, many of which were created for just such an eventuality. The Scourging could tip the balance, but the sorcerer might be able to tear through them, if Huron is busy with Verngar.

If everything works out well for Huron, he should be able to put down any sort of mutiny from Verngar with ease. However, it would not take many factors shifting by much for his hold on power to be wrenched loose. It will all come down to what Verngar's intentions are, and which way any of the parties involved would lend their support.

Huron quickens his pace a little, to make sure he reaches the cave mouth before the former Angel Encarmine. Yariel waits there, and Huron can see from his face that he can sense the tension in the air. That would make sense: you cannot spend thousands of years in the Black Legion and not be able to smell a potential rebellion when one is brewing.

'How fortuitous that we should arrive at the same moment, Lord Huron!' Verngar calls as they approach each other. Then his tone turns curious. 'Are those Imperial robots? Where did you find such things?'

'Magos Dallax and her automata joined us during my most recent raid,' Huron replies. He wonders if he can detect a hint of uncertainty in the Apostate's voice. Good: if Verngar was not expecting such fearsome war machines in Huron's retinue then it might make him reconsider any rash action, and

Huron vehemently dislikes fights where the other party has chosen the ground or the timing.

'A fine addition to our numbers,' Verngar says, with what certainly sounds like approval.

'Indeed,' Turazan agrees. It should not be possible for a Mark IV helmet to look covetous, and yet the warpsmith's manages it.

'This is our destination?' Huron demands, as he and his escort come to Yariel's side.

'The information I have suggests that the Ebon Talon rests within,' Verngar agrees.

'Your information *suggests?*' Huron repeats. He flexes the fingers of the Tyrant's Claw. Regardless of whether or not he wishes to let on that he suspects betrayal, he would be angered by the notion that this deployment could have been for nothing.

'We know that the words of daemons can be deceiving,' Verngar replies smoothly. 'That was why I was going to undertake this mission myself, lord, so as not to bring anyone down with me should I have been misled.' He comes to a halt, just out of range of a lunging strike. 'I am happy to proceed with only my companions, should you be uncertain of what awaits.'

Huron shakes his head. 'I am here. Whatever is in there is mine, and I will not stand by and make my warriors fetch it for me.'

He does not wait for Verngar to reply, and turns to lead the way into the cave, picking his way around and under the jagged spikes of glass. His huscarls form up around him once more, and the kastelans' powerful lumens ignite and cut through the darkness, causing Huron's shadow to stretch out in front of him as the beams play across his back. The walls, floor and ceiling all glitter and shine in the light, but there is a darkness to the glass here which prevents the beams from penetrating far into it.

The cave leads into the mountain, and remains roughly the same height and width, but the curve it makes to the left takes them out of sight of the outside, and Huron's vox fades into static as the reports from outside die with the signal that brings them to him. The river of blood down the centre of the cavern still runs swift and deep, but Huron pays it little mind. He has seen stranger things on such warp-twisted worlds, and it is neither use nor hindrance to him. He wonders if its presence is at all tantalising for Verngar, and smiles grimly at the thought.

'Bones,' Rafken says, and points. Huron follows his huscarl's gesture, and sees them, illuminated and pale against the dark, reflective floor. Skulls and skeletons, scattered here and there: not piled up, as might be done by devotees of the Blood God, but left where they fell.

'A predator?' Dallax asks.

'More likely a guardian of some sort,' Verngar replies, before Huron can speak. The Apostate is not far behind, but his warriors have not fully mingled with Huron's yet. There is still a faint buffer between the two groups. 'This is encouraging.'

'How is it encouraging?' Dallax demands. Her manner towards Verngar is not as deferential as it is towards Huron, which pleases the Blood Reaver. 'What is encouraging about such a danger?'

'It implies that there is something worth guarding,' Verngar says, with a chuckle. 'Come now, magos – think logically.'

'And what if we are unable to overcome this guardian?' Dallax says. 'That is not an impossibility, given the incomplete data we currently possess, and would not be a desirable outcome.'

'Then we will die on this miserable world,' Huron rasps.

'Something which I have no intention of doing.' He frowns. 'Douse the lights.'

Dallax makes her kastelans oblige, and those few Red Corsairs who had lit their own lamp packs do the same. Huron's enhanced vision adapts immediately to the new darkness, and confirms what he thought he had already seen: a faint glow from ahead.

'We surely haven't passed through the mountain already,' Yariel comments.

'That isn't sunlight,' Huron confirms. 'I suspect our goal lies ahead of us. Onwards!'

Lights spring up again, and their party sets forward once more. Now Huron hears the footsteps of Verngar and his warriors begin to quicken, almost imperceptibly. He matches them, determined not to let them get ahead of him, but without breaking into what serves him as a run these days. He can still move faster than a mortal, but his motion is lurching and laboured compared to an uninjured Space Marine, and the whole point of being Huron Blackheart is that he does not *have* to run.

They cross a threshold and the cave widens out, and suddenly the light – which had moments before still only been a glimmer – now fills this new cavern with a radiance almost that of a sunlit day on a planet outside of the Maelstrom. The source is easy to determine: somehow, despite casting the light, the curved black spike the length of Huron's forearm remains clear, dark and distinct.

'The Ebon Talon, I presume,' Huron mutters. He can feel the power radiating from it. Whatever this thing truly is, and whatever its purpose might be, it is certainly potent. A cautious man might hesitate before approaching such an oddity, but it has been many centuries since Lugft Huron could be described as a mere man, and while caution has its place, it is not here and now. He came here to claim this artefact, and that is what he intends to do: it might strip his soul from his body, or his flesh from his bones, but if he were fearful of such fates then he would never have made his home in the Maelstrom.

They come roaring out of tunnels on the far side of the cavern: three of them, each the size of a Contemptor Dreadnought, but moving with the speed and precision of an apex predator. They are monstrosities of flesh upon which the Changer of Ways has wrought his works, things that are recognisable as formerly human only in the sense of their bipedal stance, and they are attacking.

There is no need for shouted commands, no fatal moments frozen in indecision or alarm. Heretic Astartes are Astartes still, scions of the purest soldiers ever bred by humanity, and no warriors in whose veins the Emperor's ancient alchemy flows will be less than swift to join combat. Weapons are aimed and discharged before the guardian creatures are halfway across the floor: a hail of bolt-shells, the chatter of Frakn's reaper autocannon and the spitting blast of plasma from Tarmogren's weapon. All shots are placed with unwavering accuracy despite the surprise of the foes' appearance and the speed of their movement, but they achieve very little. Most are shrugged off harmlessly by the glowing aura that surrounds each beast.

Huron's lip curls. Warp sorcery can be most tiresome when it is in the service of others.

'Garvak!' Verngar yells, syllables which mean nothing to Huron for a moment, until his memory throws up an association just as the closest beast smashes into Yariel's squad. *Pridan Garvak, formerly of the Death Strike Chapter, and a member of their Librarius.* That must be the sorcerer; a turncoat of Dorn's lineage. Huron hopes that despite having betrayed his former brethren, Garvak proves to be as resolute as them.

The first guardian, pale-skinned and two-headed, swats Yariel aside and snatches up one of his men. The seized Corsair struggles against the two massive hands, each one the size of his torso, but ceramite splinters and cracks beneath the creature's fingers, and he is wrenched apart even as his companions' bolt-shells continue to bounce off the guardian's hide.

'Enough!' Huron bellows, his vocal modulator overloading and turning the word into a metallic screech. He steps forward just as the guardian leans down and reaches out for another victim, and the monstrous hand's fingertips brush against his breastplate. Huron slips to one side, guided by the dark whispers of the warp, and the guardian's questing fingers miss him. He could unleash the power of his heavy flamer now, but that is not his intent. Instead he takes one more step, then swings upwards with the Tyrant's Claw.

The thunderous uppercut catches the guardian under its left-hand chin. That head snaps backwards and the body follows, twisting and falling, but time has slowed for Huron, and he can already see the creature splaying out its arms to catch itself. The force of his blow has rocked it backwards, but it has not really been harmed. He readies his axe to strike. Sorcerous protection has its limits, and the gods are fickle. What individual power alone cannot achieve, persistence can.

Something erupts into roaring, blinding white fury to his right. Huron recognises the heavy phosphor blasters of Dallax's kastelans opening up, but the momentary distraction costs him: the guardian he just struck pivots its body to get its arms and legs under it, and as it does so, a mace-tipped tail Huron had not even seen thumps into him.

The impact lifts him clean off his feet and sends him sprawling, his armour drawing forth a screeching sound like tortured souls as it scrapes across the cavern's glass floor. The pain hits him a moment later: too much even for his bioengineering to suppress, and potent enough to register over the background agony that is his default existence. His right arm has lost power, and were his weapon there not an integral part of it, it would have slipped from his grasp. He has kept hold of his power axe, but the rest of his body refuses to move for a moment.

Triads of spots float in front of his eyes, mocking his weakness. Pain is a familiar enemy for him, but it is still an enemy. He can endure more now than in the days when he answered to the Emperor, but it still limits him. If only he were hardier and more enduring; if only pain was but a memory that need never haunt his waking days again, or better yet, was something in which he could take solace…

'You're going to have to do better than that,' Huron growls, half to the artefact's guardian, and half to the Plague Lord who seeks to tempt him with promises of greater resilience. He levers himself back to his feet, leaning heavily on his power axe to do so.

The sorcerer Garvak is surrounded by a nimbus of light as he draws on the plentiful power of the warp, but whatever he is doing has not yet had a visible effect: the guardians are still laying waste to the Red Corsairs. Even as Huron watches, the one farthest from him shoots yard-long spines out of its hide, which punch clean through the power armour of some of Verngar's followers. One falls as his head is skewered; another dies as multiple organs are pierced; a third is consumed by fire as his armour's power pack is penetrated and detonates. Verngar and Turazan are evading the creature for now, and shooting at it with plasma pistol and the arcane energies wielded by their mechatendrils, respectively, but they will be forced to either close with it or flee before long.

Dallax's kastelans are concentrating their fire on the middle creature, and their punishing salvos have driven it to one knee, but the magos has miscalculated: as her charges step forward to press the attack they approach too close to the guardian, which lunges up to seize one of the automata and hurl it into another, sending them both to the ground. Dallax steps back again, firing her gamma pistol, but although its skin is blackened and blistered the guardian begins to wade through the firepower of the remaining three robots and their mistress, intent on bringing the rest of them down.

Frakn's autocannon has run dry and he hurls himself at the nearest guardian, the one which sent Huron flying, and swings at it with his power fist. The beast swats his blow aside contemptuously and brings its own fist down on Frakn's head, crushing his trophy racks and driving the mighty warrior down to his knees. Tagron's punch lands in the guardian's solar plexus and staggers it, but its return kick flattens not only the huscarl but the two Corsairs behind him.

'Get up!' Huron snarls at Yariel, who lies some twenty yards from him. The champion's right greave is shattered, and quite possibly the limb beneath as well. 'Ten thousand years of war, and now you're going to lie there whining?'

The Blood Reaver turns his back on the former Black Legionnaire and limps back towards the combat. The mechanical miracle that is the right-hand side of his body is beginning to repair itself, as circuits bypass broken connections and systems reroute. It will not be perfect, but it never was: all it has to be is good enough. The Hamadrya appears, scampering along behind him, and Huron taps into its connection to the warp. Brute force will not be enough to bring this enemy down: he will need to take it apart, and for that he needs understanding.

The world darkens in his vision, and so does the guardian. It is now a towering thing of heavy shadow, but Huron can see the pulsing lines of power that run through it, and the nodal points where they are anchored in its flesh. They would be undetectable to the mortal eye, and a blow that struck one by chance and made a telling hit on the creature might be accounted a lucky shot, but Huron knows better. Tzeentch may delight in the paths of chance, but even the servants of the Great Changer follow systems and patterns. The mightiest bastions can fall if their weak points are known, and now Huron has the information he needs.

He weighs his power axe in his hand as he approaches, waiting for the correct moment. Centuries ago, Huron would have prefaced his attack with an inspiring battle cry invoking the Emperor. In certain circumstances, he still does, albeit to call for His death. Such a thing would be pointless here, but old habits die hard.

'This is going to hurt!' he snarls. Hurt him, hurt the guardian, hurt anyone nearby. Whatever is necessary.

There.

The guardian turns, bringing both of its fists down in a devastating double hammer blow on the already prone Frakn, and Huron has his opening. He swings, and his power axe slices down to cut into the meat of the guardian's monstrously swollen right shoulder, penetrating the sorcerous aura around it for the first time.

One.

The guardian roars in pain and rage, and whirls around in an attempt to backhand Huron. He ducks just enough for the savage swipe to miss his head, and lands his axe into the flesh over the guardian's right ribs.

Two.

He sidesteps a downward blow of the thing's left fist and cuts up at its other shoulder, and once more his axe strikes home and severs another node of power.

Three.

Tail…!

He is too slow. The tail strikes him again – only a glancing blow this time, but still enough to bowl him over. He feels a surge of power as Garvak finally gets off whatever incantation he's been working on – something complex and potent from the feel of it, no wonder it took a while – and the shriek from the far side of the cavern suggests that it has met with success.

'Left eye of the right-hand head!' Huron bawls, clambering back to his feet again. 'Shoot it out!'

His remaining warriors do not waste time demanding to know why that specific point, or questioning why it should work when their attacks have barely registered so far. A fusillade of bolter fire roars out, concentrated on that one spot no matter how the guardian moves, and Huron's altered vision sees it flare and go dark.

Four.

The guardian howls, a cry of pain and rage that ascends through the octaves until Huron feels like his very bones are vibrating. However, the pause while he recovered himself has given his bionics the chance to finish adjusting to their damage, and the Tyrant's Claw is once more under his control. He steps in and lashes out to slam it home into the left-hand side of the guardian's chest.

Five.

The creature staggers, and its fist bounces off instead of

flattening Huron when he uses the Tyrant's Claw to parry its desperate return swing.

'Right knee!'

Tarmogren's plasma gun spits, and the joint disappears in a bolt of ravening energy.

Six.

The guardian swings for Huron's head again, this time with its right hand, and his counter blow with his power axe shears it clean off at the wrist.

Seven.

'Base of the tail!' he barks. A guttural war cry goes up, and Huron catches a glimpse of Yariel using his one good leg to throw himself at the guardian's back, chainsword held in both hands. The blade bites home, and the penultimate node of power winks out in Huron's vision.

Eight.

The guardian stumbles, drops to one knee, and sweeps out one massive hand to try to brace itself. Its heads are finally within easy reach, even for a battered old warrior relying on a body made of abused flesh and damaged bionics. Huron raises his power axe and brings it down with all the force he can muster, right where the two necks meet the body.

The blade *thunks* into the altered flesh and buries itself to the haft, sizzling and spitting as the power field distorts and breaks down the matter with which it is in contact. The guardian lets out a last, wordless moan, and topples backwards, so Huron turns to assess the rest of the combat.

Frakn is almost certainly dead, and only three of Yariel's squad are still in one piece, not counting the champion himself. Two of Magos Dallax's kastelans lie in shattered ruins, and the magos herself is moving with the air of one whose body is partially broken – an air Huron knows all too well – but the guardian her charges were fighting is now a blackened, smouldering and pulverised wreck. Less than half of Verngar's honour guard have survived, but Turazan and Pridan Garvak are still in one piece, and the guardian they had been fighting has been crushed by what appears to have been a spell not dissimilar to the one the native sorcerer used to kill the Raptors. And Verngar himself…

Is stepping up to the plinth on which rests the Ebon Talon.

'Verngar!' Huron barks, wrenching his power axe free and stepping towards his underling and the artefact. Verngar's hands are already outstretched, however, and they close on the Talon before Huron can take a second stride, or utter another word.

'For your glory, Lord Huron!' the Apostate bellows in tones both joyful and insincere. He snatches the Ebon Talon from its resting place and lifts it high, and Huron's mind flashes back to the images the daemon used to taunt him while he was tracking the *Macragge's Honour*.

He has no time to dwell on it, however, because above them all, something goes *crack*. In a mountain made of glass, that is not a welcome sound.

'Get us out of here!' Verngar roars, his voice abruptly much more matter-of-fact, and he throws himself towards Turazan and Garvak. Huron feels the power building almost immediately and hisses a curse, but just as he is about to get his metaphysical fingers into it, Garvak finishes his spell. The warp power rises in a tide of blue fire that obscures them from view, and when it dies down again a moment later Garvak, Turazan, Verngar and his surviving honour guard have all disappeared.

Along with the Ebon Talon.

For a moment, Huron can only stare with impotent rage at the space where they had stood. He trailed the Apostate to this miserable world, butchered his way through uncounted enemies, and still Verngar managed to lay his wretched hands on the Ebon Talon. What is more, he did so despite Huron being here. Instead of ensuring that Verngar never got his hands on the artefact, Huron has allowed him to demonstrate his superiority by claiming it. With that and the *Macragge's Honour*, Verngar will be able to sway many hearts and minds to his side.

Huron's mouth tastes like ashes, but he has no time to dwell on his fury. The mountain cracks again, and from the passage that leads back to the questionable safety of the outside comes a tinkle as of falling shards of glass.

'Lord Huron?' Tagron asks. The huscarl is breathing heavily, not a good sign in a Space Marine. 'What are your orders?'

'What do you think they are?' Huron snarls. 'Run!'

FOURTEEN

Huron Blackheart should not have to run, but now he does.

The mountain is cracking above and around him. Perhaps whatever sorcery held this unnatural pinnacle together is expiring now the Ebon Talon has been removed; perhaps it is a delayed reaction to stress fractures in the planet's crust as a result of the Red Corsairs' initial bombardment; perhaps it is simply the whim of the Changer of Ways, extending his finger from the warp to meddle with this world for his own amusement. The details are irrelevant: the floor is crazing with cracks through which the river of blood is beginning to drain, glass is falling from above, and Huron intends to be outside before anything more substantial can land on his head.

What he will do out there is another matter entirely, since he doubts that the mountainside will be a particularly safe place, but even the greatest strategists sometimes have to deal with one thing at a time.

The Hamadrya chitters a warning, and Huron jinks to one side just in time to avoid a chunk of glass as big as him that falls and shatters, spraying glittering shrapnel in all directions. He raises one hand to shield his face, and hears the shards clattering off his armour, and that of his remaining warriors.

They round the curve in the tunnel, and now he can see the light of outside. However, a crack races along the glass ceiling above his head, faster than any of them are running, and it terminates at the cave mouth.

Which falls in.

Massive chunks of glass begin to fall, piling up and blocking the exit. The burning anger in Huron's heart grows as the eerie light of Kyren's skies fades, and he casts every curse he can think of into the warp, in the general direction of Verngar the Apostate.

Mighty footsteps overtake him, and he realises that two of Griza Dallax's remaining kastelans are pounding ahead, their strides lengthening until they leave the rest of the group behind. As soon as they reach the blockade they set to work, battering at it with their energised fists in rapid one-two motions that not even an Adeptus Astartes warrior could hope to emulate. Shards of glass fly in all directions, but the automata pay them no mind, and to Huron's astonishment, there is already a chink of light leaking in by the time he catches up with the pair of robots.

'Afraid of the dark, magos?' He laughs.

'Darkness can be a hindrance to certain functions, and can leave an unaugmented human vulnerable to predators or enemies with more sensitive light-processing equipment, but fear of darkness in and of itself would be irrational,' Dallax replies, over the sound of her charges pulverising their way through a wall of glass. Her third kastelan is behind her for some reason, instead of joining in the excavation, but the light of its lumen means it is only a dark shape to Huron, even with his enhanced eyesight. He wonders for a moment whether she is planning for it to attack him, but he disregards the notion immediately. She cannot hope to leave this world without him, so why set her robots to digging at all if she intends treachery?

He does not reply to Dallax's statement: he has no fear of anything, but being crushed to death by a mountain is one of the more ignominious ends he can think of, so it seems pointless to aggravate her at this moment. A huge hunk of glass is smashed in two and the debris knocked aside, and what is revealed is a gap large enough for every individual in their party to fit through. One of the kastelans braces itself to prevent other chunks of dislodged glass from falling into the gap and barring their way once more, and the other squeezes through.

'There is still a traversable surface outside,' Dallax reports.

'Good.' Huron follows the kastelan out and activates his vox, which coughs into life with the usual confusion of noise and shouting that accompanies any warzone. 'This is Blackheart. *Bloodstrike*, come in.'

There are a few moments while his vox crackles emptily, providing nothing more than snippets of exchanges between his warriors on the glass plains below. Then, as his huscarls follow him, Huron hears Carazzalan's voice in his ear.

'Bloodstrike *here, Lord Huron. Do you require extraction?*'

'I do,' Huron tells the Mechanicum adept grimly. The remnants of The Scourging are making their way out now, including Yariel, who caught up to them while they waited for the kastelans to clear their exit. The first of the automata is heading towards the path up which they came. It makes sense to Huron: send the heaviest first, and see if the ground holds. 'We are on the mountainside. Make all haste, because it's starting to collapse under us.'

'Acknowledged, lord. Can you provide any details of your location?'

'The only details you need are that I'm going to tell the *Spectre* that if you don't find me before this mountain falls down, it is to vaporise you and that craft you're piloting!' Huron snarls. 'Do I make myself clear?'

'...Yes, lord.'

'Good!' Huron switches channels to a general broadcast. 'This is Blackheart. We've got what we came for, and the mountain is growing less stable. Commence withdrawal immediately.'

He does not wait for any acknowledgement. His commanders know what they have to do: any that have a desperate wish to stay and slaughter more of the natives are not worth his time in any case.

'Never mind the mountain, lord,' Tagron says, pointing. 'Look there!'

Huron follows his huscarl's gesture, and sees a dark, jagged line running across the planet's surface which, his memory tells him, was not there during their ascent.

'Fickle are the ways of the warp,' he mutters.

'Is the surface going to be any safer than the heights?' Dallax's voice asks, and Huron turns to address her. However, his words die on his lips as he sees what her third kastelan, the one which took no part in excavating their exit from the cave, is carrying in its arms.

Frakn's Terminator-armoured form is dwarfed by the battle robot, and the mighty warrior looks almost like a child. Huron had been so focused on getting out of the cavern that he had not noticed the automata's burden.

'He still lives?' he asked, astonished.

'I detect no life signs from his armour, lord,' Dallax replies. 'However, damaged although it is, such a suit is a valuable relic – far more so than the power armour worn by the other casualties. I presumed you would wish it to be salvaged.'

Frakn had been an Astral Claw, and there were few enough of them left now: one fewer, after today. Huron Blackheart is not a warrior prone to sentiment, especially given what his Chapter once represented and who they served, but he still does not relish the thought of a day when there are none left who once wore the silver and blue.

His huscarl's body will not be desecrated. Huron knows all too well that there is little enough peace to be found in the warp, but he will do his best to see that whatever can be achieved is what Frakn will get. Then his armour will be repaired, so far as possible, and awarded to another worthy candidate.

'You have done well, magos,' is all Huron says as he turns away to hurry after the leading automata. 'As for the surface, I cannot say what it will be like should we get there, but I know that it is *not* safe here.'

'Acknowledged, lord.'

'That is loyalty, lord,' Tagron's voice speaks into Huron's ear, on the private vox-channel between Huron and his huscarls. 'So far as I am concerned, it has earned her a favour from us.'

'Agreed,' Huron subvocalises back, his voice so low that not even Dallax's auditory sensors would be able to pick it up. 'Should Turazan or any of his ilk attempt to interfere with her, instruct them to seek their amusements elsewhere.'

'What about the Alchemancer, lord? The others might respect our words on your behalf, but he will only listen to you.'

Huron grunts. 'I will talk to Valthex. I suspect she would be beneath his notice in any case. Of course, this is predicated on us actually getting off this warp-cursed planet...'

The engines of a Stormbird are powerful, however, even after ten millennia of service. A dot in the sky swells to become the shape of *Bloodstrike*, and Huron releases a gout of flame from the Tyrant's Claw to signal their location. The attack craft decelerates as it approaches, and Carazzalan expertly guides it so that the tip of the ramp is just nudging against the edge of the path, while the nose of the craft looms above them.

An Imperial commander might have ushered his underlings on first, holding to the axioms of being the last to withdraw. Huron has no time for such foolishness, and boards first. His safety is paramount; the rest of his warband are, ultimately, expendable. That is one reason why he is still alive, and why so many of his enemies are not.

They are all aboard, and *Bloodstrike* is burning hard for orbit, when Magos Dallax lets out a binharic bleat of what Huron interprets as alarm.

'What ails you, magos?' he enquires.

'Check the sensor readings, Lord Huron,' is all she says. He does so, patching through to *Bloodstrike*'s readings.

Kyren is coming apart.

The fissures he saw in the surface were not just cosmetic: they now extend hundreds of miles downwards. The entire planet is shattering, as some destructive force overpowers whatever hold gravity has on it. The mountain in which the Ebon Talon rested is long gone, already tumbled into an abyss that opened at its foot. Every life remaining on Kyren's surface is doomed.

'Blood of the gods,' Yariel says softly. 'Was that thing holding the entire planet together?'

Huron does not know. But the mere possibility of an artefact with that much potential power being in the hands of anyone other than him is not a situation he relishes; and yet it is the one in which he finds himself.

'Signal ahead to the *Spectre of Ruin*,' he instructs Carazzalan. 'As soon as transports are aboard, I want us making full speed back to New Badab. We *will* get there before the *Macragge's Honour*.'

FIFTEEN

The war room in the Palace of Thorns hums with tension, but it is not the excited tension of a strategy council, where warriors plan for victory and the downfall of their enemies, all while being cognisant of the possibility of their own death. Or perhaps it is, but on this occasion, some of the enemies are in the same room.

Armenneus Valthex has kept his own counsel since the return of the expedition to Kyren, and his counsel has not been sought. Now he stands at one side of the master tactical hololith generator and glances back and forth between the two mighty figures who stand opposed across it.

On his right, Verngar the Apostate. A former Angel Encarmine, and a warrior in his prime. The captor and gaoler of Roboute Guilliman, although admittedly not for long. The Lord of the Talon, as whispers have named him; the one who claimed the powerful artefact known as the Ebon Talon from the warp-twisted world of Kyren, and returned triumphant in the mighty plundered warship the *Macragge's Honour*.

On Valthex's left, Huron Blackheart, the Blood Reaver. An old and battered commander whose body has been failing him for a century, and who appears to be held together with spite, malice and dark sorcery. Huron's stubborn refusal to die is enough to garner admiration even from those who find themselves at odds with him, but Valthex is no longer certain that admiration is going to be enough to stave off the hounds of ambition. The *Spectre of Ruin* emerged from the depths of the warp at the same time as the *Macragge's Honour*, but only a fool would think their respective captains were still working in concert.

Verngar has brought lackeys with him. Valthex recognises the sorcerer Pridan Garvak, and behind him are Deinos Kinkiller, Euryphycus of the Severed Hand, the Skintaker, and others. It is a none-too-subtle demonstration of power, and it is a challenge to Huron's authority.

A challenge that the Blood Reaver seems not to have recognised.

'The first reports from the assault on Chogoris are promising,' Huron rasps, gesturing to the hololith. Valthex does not need to concentrate to see that the statement is correct.

'It surprises me that it has been so easy,' Deinos Kinkiller remarks. 'Assaulting a Chapter's home world would normally be suicide, particularly that of a First Founding Chapter.'

'Chogoris has never truly embraced the Imperium's technology,' Valthex replies. 'They prefer their traditional ways. Presumably the White Scars themselves find this appealing since they can continue to rule as warrior gods, much as the Space Wolves do on Fenris. I imagine that it is easier to indoctrinate potential acolytes if they are already half-convinced of your divinity.' He shakes his head. Why deliberately keep your people ignorant and struggling? Once you accepted that there was no higher intelligence governing the Imperium – that the will of the Emperor was a myth, and the High Lords of Terra were nothing more than greedy, corrupt humans – so many of its lies and hypocrisies were laid bare.

'Regardless of the reasons, Chogoris is struggling,' Huron continues. 'Prayd has done well. The whispers carried on the warp suggest that the White Scars are withdrawing from Armageddon to counter our attack, which gives us an opportunity.' He smiles, exposing sharp teeth. 'Jubal Khan might well expect an ambush, but he'll still have no choice except to walk into the trap, unless he wants to see his world slaughtered.'

'I have an addendum, Lord Huron,' Verngar says.

The Blood Reaver looks up. He has rarely seemed more alone, Valthex realises. Huron's huscarls are outside the chamber to protect from external threats, not from their master's closest advisors. Corpsemaster Garreon is still at Hell's Iris, Turazan and Garlon Souleater are absent, studying the Ebon Talon aboard the *Macragge's Honour* – an invitation which was not extended to Valthex – and Prayd and Garrix are of course prosecuting the war on Chogoris. Of all the senior voices within the Red Corsairs, only Valthex himself still stands here next to his master.

And he is not precisely *next* to him.

Armenneus Valthex is loyal, but he is realistic. Huron Blackheart turned his back on the Imperium because it was weak. If Blackheart loses his grip on the mighty force he now commands, is he not weak himself? This the Maelstrom, after all, where the most the weak can hope for is a swift death. If Huron cannot hold onto his power, does he deserve it?

'You do, Verngar?' Huron asks. He has still not acknowledged the presence of Verngar's followers, other than to respond to Deinos' remark. Perhaps he thinks that to comment on them will make him look insecure, but Valthex worries that they are past that point now. Verngar is starting to take liberties, confident he has enough support to face Huron down if it comes to it. Huron should have barred that support from the war room, unless he had specifically requested their presence. To pretend there is no problem is a sign that you cannot solve it.

'Kor'sarro Khan is pulling back from the Second Agrellan Campaign,' Verngar states. 'The Khan uses our attack on his home world as an excuse to flee. His forces will be coming in damaged and demoralised from the beating they took at the hands of the t'au, but also desperate, and a desperate enemy can be the most dangerous.' Verngar spreads his hands and smiles. 'If we were preparing for one enemy, we might have been routed by the sudden appearance of another. However, if we are ready for both, we can spring an appropriate trap.'

Valthex would dearly like to find out how Verngar knows about Agrellan. Huron spoke of the whispers of the warp; does the Apostate have similar resources now? If he has made the same sort of pacts with the Dark Gods as Huron, the Blood Reaver's time might be short indeed. The Hamadrya flickers into visibility on Huron's shoulders, currently taking the form of a reptilian with grasping hands, but Valthex can see no sign of Verngar being disconcerted by the familiar's appearance.

'I will draw up tactical options for variables on Mandeville point arrivals for our foes, strength and disposition of their forces, and their arrival times,' Valthex offers, but he does not direct the comment so much as speak it into the air.

'Thank you, Alchemancer,' Verngar replies, glancing at him. 'Your assistance is appreciated.'

Valthex can read the subtext into that statement without

difficulty. His aid is something else that Verngar seeks to claim, silently daring Huron to stop him. Furthermore, Valthex is being reminded that his position in any version of the Red Corsairs with Verngar at the helm is only secure so long as he is of use.

For a moment, Valthex considers responding with force to Verngar's veiled threats, but he dismisses the notion instantly. Verngar is a fierce combatant, and Valthex's most potent weapon – the conversion beamer he has incorporated into the Indynabula Array – is of limited use against a target such as a fellow Space Marine, who could easily react in the second or so it takes to power up to fire. No, if Valthex is to take action against the Apostate then it will need to be something subtler, and Verngar will likely be on his guard, since there are few more paranoid than those planning a betrayal.

'With your leave, Lord Huron,' Verngar says, 'I will assemble a fleet suitable to reinforce our brothers in the Chogoris System, and prepare for the arrival of–'

'No.'

Huron's single word is harsh and rasped, but it cuts through Verngar's smooth tones like a knife through flesh.

Verngar raises his eyebrows. 'No?'

The Apostate is still wavering on just the correct side of decorum, insofar as these things are measured in a warband of heretics, but it is a very fine line indeed. Valthex is centuries old now, with plenty of experience of keeping his physical responses under tight control, but even he can feel his body preparing for action. Huron has chosen the place in which he is making his stand, and everything now depends on how Verngar reacts.

'I will assemble the fleet,' Huron says bluntly. 'I will command it. I am not some Alpha Legion puppet master, to hide behind others. Prayd has set the lure – now I will set the trap.'

'Lord, I would ask you to reconsider,' Verngar says. Behind him, the Skintaker shifts, his hands straying to the two long xenos blades he wears on his hips. 'Let me command the fleet, and in your name I will crush these First Founding whelps and let our name ring out across the stars. I retrieved the Ebon Talon – I did not fail you.'

Valthex has heard of how that happened; how Verngar seized the artefact and fled with his sorcerer, leaving Huron to escape from a collapsing mountain as best he could. It tastes like rank cowardice in Valthex's mouth, but there is logic to it nonetheless: better to get the artefact clear so the Red Corsairs can use it, than risk it being lost along with all those who had gone to claim it. Huron should not have needed rescuing. For the Blood Reaver to comment on Verngar's abandonment of him will be to highlight his own weakness.

'You did,' Huron acknowledges. 'But you have never been a planetary governor, Verngar, nor have you have ever been Chapter Master. Your experience of command has not yet stretched to a warzone that encompasses an entire system. I have overseen operations in many.' Huron shakes his head defiantly. 'The planet lacks technological advancement over much of it, but it is still an Astartes home world, and those returning to it and defending it will know it better than we ever can. This is not the place for you to get your first taste of such command.'

Valthex sees a glance or two directed at the back of Verngar's head by his lackeys. They are hungry for battle and glory, but only the first is guaranteed against the White Scars, who are masters of lightning warfare. Huron's tactical nous is well known. Verngar's star might be rising, but he has not proven himself in the same manner. If Verngar decides to force the issue, it will come down to a choice: do these warriors trust him not to lead them to defeat? Huron's gambit is bold, but not necessarily unwise.

Verngar sidesteps it.

'What, then, if we take a different approach?' the Apostate suggests. He pulls back the hololith until it shows a large portion of the galaxy once more, complete with icons marking the last-known locations of all major forces, be they Imperial, Chaos or xenos. Verngar highlights a new planet: one closer to the Maelstrom than Chogoris.

'Ogrys?' Valthex queries. A touch of a rune brings up the relevant data, which begins to scroll past in line after line of glyphs.

'The ruined home world of the Invaders Chapter,' Verngar says. 'Practically on our way to Chogoris. The Imperium is attempting to rebuild, but their efforts have been interrupted by the Great Rift.' He smiles. 'Let me take command of the fleet, Lord Huron, and not only will I show you that I can subjugate an Astartes home world, but also we will arrive at Chogoris better supplied than when we leave the Maelstrom.'

Valthex takes a moment to study the data on Ogrys. It is indeed designated as the Invaders' home world, but if the information is correct – and that is never a completely safe assumption, with the Imperium – then it is still recovering from a devastating attack by the aeldari of the Alaitoc craftworld, and the Chapter are currently fleet-based. Ogrys is relatively lightly defended, but being stocked ready for use by a Space Marine Chapter in the future: there could be few more tempting targets for the Red Corsairs.

Here is the new trap for Huron. To refuse such an easy target will make it clear that he fears Verngar gaining more power, but to take Verngar up on his offer will very likely let the Apostate get another notable triumph to his name, and means he will almost certainly lead the action in Chogoris. Once that happens, Huron's days in command will be finished.

Huron taps his fingers on the hololith table for a moment, then looks up at Verngar. 'How is the *Macragge's Honour* responding?'

'Very well,' Verngar replies, with a broad smile. 'The machine-spirit is proving more tractable than you feared.'

'Excellent,' Huron says. 'Given that, I will be taking it as my flagship.'

Verngar's smile freezes.

'You can lead the assault on Ogrys, Lord Verngar,' Huron tells him. 'And I will be there assessing your competence, to see whether I am prepared to let you handle matters at Chogoris.' He taps a rune, and the hololith winks out. 'Dismissed, all of you.'

For a moment, Valthex is sure that Verngar is going to stage his coup here and now: activate Stormfiend, lunge for the Blood Reaver and seek to take his power along with his head. But then the Apostate's smile returns to life, and he bows, and he withdraws with his companions. After all, Huron has just given him everything he asked for.

Valthex does not leave with the others. He waits until the door has shut behind them and then turns to Huron, but the Blood Reaver speaks first.

'Are you going to warn me about his ambition again, Armenneus?'

'I doubt that you need my warning to see it, lord,' Valthex says. 'What concerns me is how you intend to deal with it, for it is clear to me that he intends to see you reduced to a figurehead before he supplants you.'

'Ambition is a good quality, in moderation,' Huron rasps. 'Hubris, however, is not. Verngar has an overabundance of both, and it will cost him.'

'You are waiting for him to fail, and he never fails enough for it to count,' Valthex says. He is speaking openly, more openly than he might have normally dared, but he is worried. Huron Blackheart is a monster; he is vicious, vindictive and ruthless. He is also, in Valthex's eyes, preferable to Verngar the Apostate. 'While you wait for the correct moment to strike, he is preparing a position from which your strike will be blunted!'

'Do not presume to lecture me in matters of war, Forgemaster!' Huron spits, rounding on Valthex with a snarl, and suddenly the broken-down old warrior is gone, replaced by a scar-visaged creature of malice around whom the dark winds of sorcery swirl. Valthex stands his ground, but the sheer hatred he sees in the Blood Reaver's eyes gives him pause, even though he suspects – and hopes – that he is not its target.

'I am not beaten,' Huron seethes, although Valthex feels that having to proclaim such a fact calls into doubt its veracity. 'Verngar is a child, who thinks that because he has spent a couple of decades living in the Maelstrom, he understands everything. His comprehension is limited, and his lack of perspective makes him both predictable and vulnerable.' The Hamadrya chitters from his shoulder, and Huron smiles, and speaks the words that Armenneus Valthex hoped he would never hear.

'I still have one last bargain I can make. I will be in my chambers. Do not interrupt me if you value your soul.'

SIXTEEN

Ogrys was once considered a safe distance from the Maelstrom, but the appearance of the Great Rift has changed that. Nightmares, hallucinations and other less easily explicable phenomena have risen in frequency ever since the great green scar ripped across the sky, and ghosts and the occasional dead-eyed revenant have troubled the unhappy populace, when once such stories would have been dismissed as children's tales.

And yet, humans are nothing if not adaptable. Despair gripped the planet in the first crushing days of the Noctis Aeterna, when hope seemed lost, but despair is not a state that can persist perpetually: a mind either breaks, or it evolves to cope in some fashion. Those who survived the initial panics found a way to live with their new reality, and as the dark tide subsided and word began to seep back in from the wider Imperium, new hope flowered. Not only was Ogrys no longer alone, but Roboute Guilliman was returned, and leading a crusade to rekindle the fires of the Imperium!

So it is that when the *Macragge's Honour* emerges from the warp, the initial reaction of those monitoring the planet's auspexes is one of unbridled joy. It takes several seconds before they realise that the ships that are translating with it are not Ultramarines vessels, or even part of some wider task force. Most of them *were* Imperial ships, once, and their shapes and classes can still be identified, but they no longer serve their old masters. Now they are the riders on the wings of the storm.

And they bring the storm with them.

As the Red Corsairs fleet bears down on the Laskar-class star fort *Emperor's Eye*, which holds station around Ogrys' moon, the defenders find the stars blurring. The multicoloured smudge of the Maelstrom, which has grown to be the brightest point in the sky other than the system's star, almost seems to be laughing at them.

Gunnery Officer Dantus Yiber scowls desperately at his screen, where despite a blizzard of contacts, his targeting system resolutely refuses to lock onto any of them. He desperately whispers the hymn of accuracy, and administers a ritual blow to the side of the cogitator – he is no tech-priest of Mars, but you don't work on the guns for thirty years without picking up a few things – but to no avail. He cannot even make the machine-spirit realise that what's in front of it are things it should be shooting at, let alone get it to select an actual target.

'Fire!' bellows his comm-bead. *'Fire!'*

'The machine-spirit isn't responding!' Dantus replies, and now his ear is alive with other voices, reporting the same issues. The *Emperor's Eye* has weapons crewed by servitors as well as gunners like him, but judging by the clipped, buzzing reports of Overseer-Magos Hecute, their systems are having no more joy than his.

'I don't care what the machine-spirit is or isn't doing, I want those guns firing! Even if you don't hit those bastards, I want them to know we're trying!'

'Yes, sir,' Dantus mutters, hastily running through the direct firing protocol in his mind. He has never done it outside of training: he has to placate the targeting spirit before it will let him shoot without a confirmed lock; then he will need to traverse the weapon manually using the pitch and yaw controls, which he is suddenly not sure received their dose of unguents during the last maintenance ritual…

He glances up and out of the viewport at the specks of light that make up the attacking fleet. They seem so small and insignificant from here, but the read-outs have told him just how much danger he is in. Behind them, the Maelstrom yawns.

And reaches out to him.

It does not move in any way Dantus Yiber can articulate: it does not grow in his vision, and its profile against the darkness beyond does not alter. Nonetheless, as he stares open-mouthed at it, he feels the brush of *something* against his consciousness. It is feather-light, a tenebrous touch that passes almost as soon as it has arrived, and when it has gone he…

He…

'Yiber! Why aren't you firing?'

What was he…?

Dantus Yiber looks down at his hands, and screams. They have not altered in any way; the skin is the same colour, and they have not grown into claws, or melted into digitless appendages. Nonetheless, he abruptly realises with a bone-deep certainty that *they are not his hands*, and they should not be on the end of his arms, and–

In Dantus' ear, the comm-bead begins to crackle with the screams of the rest of the gunnery decks. He wants to pluck it out and throw it away, but these are not his hands.

SEVENTEEN

'Resistance is light,' Verngar the Apostate declares with satisfaction. 'Just as I predicted.'

Huron Blackheart looks down on him from the shipmaster's throne. The Blood Reaver is sitting where dozens of Ultramarines heroes have sat before him, including the mighty Roboute Guilliman himself. It is a position that screams glory and authority. The person who sits here should be the unquestioned master of all they survey, from the interior of the bridge to the farthest reaches of the hololith displays that provide tactical read-outs for thousands of miles around.

And yet, Huron is not the one directing the battle. The Master of the Maelstrom sits and watches as Verngar gives orders to ships, to boarding parties and to the gunnery crews of the *Macragge's Honour*, and he watches as they obey. The star fort is already in their hands, its brief hopes of resistance overwhelmed. Two frigates have already deployed cables, ready to tow it away with them through the warp when they leave. The Red Corsairs leave nothing behind which they can use.

In truth, Verngar is not performing poorly. No Space Marine is an incompetent tactician, because this is what they are bred for: not just the close work of killing, but reading and assessing situations, and determining how best to respond. Only those totally in the grip of some other power – like the uncontrollable bloodlust of Khorne, or the sensation-seeking excesses of Slaanesh – would have their judgement impaired. Even then, that is not to say that they would not be able to shape events to their own choosing, merely that their goals would be personal satisfaction rather than a wider strategic victory.

However, there is a difference between adequacy and brilliance. Not every member of the Adeptus Astartes would make a Chapter Master. This war fleet has nearly stripped New Badab bare, but its might is not best deployed as a hammer blow. Each part, each ship, has its own role to play: especially in a fleet that flies under the banner of the Ruinous Powers, where vessels that look similar might have vastly different capabilities, and where the captains can be even more hungry for gain and glory than their counterparts in the Imperial Navy. In his past, Huron has commanded forces where he could rely on his officers to obey his orders, secure in the knowledge that they are part of the greater whole. Here, every captain knows that their reward for this battle will be only what they can carve out of Ogrys' hide. You have to understand that desire and direct it, not assume that you can overrule it.

'There are ships approaching from equatorial orbit,' Huron rasps, cutting through the steady back-and-forth of orders and responses to and from Verngar. The Apostate does not so much as glance up at him.

'They are of no consequence.'

Huron growls in his throat. 'They are positioning themselves to intercept our ships returning from looting the supply dump just south of the continent's secondary mountain range.'

'And the *Wolf of Fenris* will hold position to prevent them from doing so,' Verngar replies. His tone dips into condescending, even bored, and Huron resists the temptation to strike at him with the Tyrant's Claw. Huron's huscarls are not here, and Verngar is flanked by two Possessed: Ak'Nakrth and Guthrada, former Red Corsairs who made their own personal deals with the warp to give their bodies up to daemons. Huron does not know for sure what bargains Verngar has struck to keep them at his side instead of reddening their claws in the boarding and landing, but they are formidable bodyguards.

'The *Wolf of Fenris* is drifting out of position even as we speak,' Huron observes acidly. 'The *Vlka Fenryka* didn't turn their coats just to play nursemaid while your favourites claim the best bounties. They want blood on their teeth.' He scans the displays again. 'The *Reign of Spite* can fill the role – Captain Sargotta was Imperial Fleet, and knows blockade actions. She'll be happy to prove herself superior to these–'

'The *Wolf of Fenris* will do as I command!' Verngar roars, rounding on Huron. 'Or they will suffer the consequences!'

Huron pauses. Verngar's eyes have the light of fanaticism in them once more, and possibly the rising blood-hunger of his gene-curse, which makes for a dangerous combination. The two Possessed beside him cackle and chuckle in their distended throats, and flex their claws. The loyalty of daemons and those who are bound to them is always fickle, and Huron has little doubt that these two will heed Verngar rather than him, should it come to it.

The Hamadrya hisses at them from his shoulder, and although

their faces no longer have features on which human emotions can be properly conveyed, the faintest hint of caution enters the Possessed's stances. They can smell the sorcery on Huron, and it makes them wary.

'How will you enact your will?' Huron asks Verngar, paying no attention to the Apostate's guards. 'Will you fire on them from this ship? That could lead to all manner of confusion within our fleet, bearing in mind the former allegiance of the *Macragge's Honour*. The last thing we need is for half our captains to decide that it has thrown off your command, and is attacking them.'

Verngar grins, exposing his prominent canines. Huron can see the faintest sheen of red across the Apostate's teeth: he has indulged his thirst, and recently.

'I need no such crude mechanisms,' Verngar declares. He activates his vox and speaks into it. 'Turazan. Bring me the Talon.'

Huron hesitates.

He was certain that the secrets of the Ebon Talon had remained a mystery to Verngar. Why else would the Apostate not have headed for the Blackstone Fortress, to activate it and begin ravaging the Imperium? The webway gate at its heart could presumably be sealed or destroyed, to prevent further unwelcome guests. With such a potent weapon under his command, Verngar could have led an assault on Chogoris that even the entire White Scars Chapter would have been hard-pressed to repel.

It is possible, of course, that Kairos Fateweaver was lying; it is certainly possible that Verngar has been. The fact of the Ebon Talon's existence, and that it was located where Verngar had said it would be, does not mean it can be used for the purpose the Apostate had claimed. Perhaps the prospect of an activated Blackstone Fortress had only ever been bait.

Whether or not that is true, it seems Verngar has found *some* use for it, and that is a potential complication in an already delicate situation.

'Give me a channel to the *Wolf of Fenris,*' Verngar commands, and the vox-officer signals for him to go ahead. '*Wolf of Fenris,* you are moving away from your assigned station. Correct your course, and prepare to engage.'

The voice that replies is a growl, filled with the harsh consonants of Fenris and forced out around fangs that are longer than Verngar's own. The Space Wolves have their own gene-curse, and the Maelstrom has not treated all of them kindly.

'Kraken take you, Verngar! We're not going to sit by and let your pups get the best pickings!'

Even through his uncertainty, Huron snorts a laugh. He smiles at Verngar. 'I did tell you.'

Verngar does not reply, either to Huron or to the defiant sons of the Rout. He signals the vox-operator to cut the transmission, and sighs. 'The Ruinous Powers take all Fenrisians. They have neither the humility to follow orders, nor the wit to make themselves useful.'

Huron is going to reply, when the bridge doors open, and light enters.

He has not seen the Ebon Talon since Kyren: the artefact has been secured on the *Macragge's Honour*, being studied by Turazan and Garlon Souleater. There is no sign of the sorcerer, but the warpsmith is the one who is bearing the Talon, holding it reverentially before him between two of his mechatendrils. The Ebon Talon's light is not as bright as it was in the cavern on Kyren, where it reflected off every faceted surface, but it still washes out over the bridge of the *Macragge's Honour*. It casts strange shadows as it goes, Huron notices: shadows that do not completely match the stance of those who cast them, or which move a fraction before or a moment after they should.

Verngar turns towards the light with a naked hunger in his face that even Huron finds perturbing, and advances towards Turazan with his arms outstretched. He seizes the Ebon Talon from the warpsmith eagerly yet tenderly, like a parent reclaiming an infant they had thought lost to them forever. Once it rests between his gauntlets, Verngar's smile nearly splits his face. Huron does not think he imagines the light getting slightly brighter as soon as the Talon is in the Apostate's grasp.

Verngar turns to the vox-officer. 'Open a channel to the fleet!'

'Aye, lord.' The crewer hastily manipulates the controls, then bows in his seat. 'Channel open.'

'Hear me, Red Corsairs!' Verngar booms, raising his voice. 'I am in command of this assault, and my orders will be obeyed! The crew of the *Wolf of Fenris* have shown themselves to be doubly disloyal, and so they will reap the consequences!'

He holds the Ebon Talon before him, one end in each hand, and begins to mutter under his breath. The light starts to grow stronger.

'Verngar!' Huron shouts, rising from his throne. 'Cease this folly!'

'Sentiment from the Blood Reaver?' Verngar scoffs. 'You are weak, and your time is past!'

The crew on the bridge have not been unaware of the tension that exists between their two commanders, but they have universally dealt with it by ignoring it. That option is no longer open to them, and Huron sees hesitant glances and even a few open mouths as each person takes in the lie of the land, and tries to decide where it is best to stand.

The two Possessed, however, show no sign of conflicted loyalties. They stare Huron down, as though daring him to make a move. Nor does Turazan denounce the Apostate.

'I am not weak,' Huron grinds out. 'I am a practical man, and I abhor waste. The crew of the *Wolf of Fenris* are some of our finest assault troops – it is folly to vent your ego on them as revenge for them refusing a role to which they are not well suited!'

'The *Wolf of Fenris* is breaking formation and coming around!' someone shouts. 'They appear to be preparing for an attack run!'

That is the Vlka Fenryka all over: when faced with a threat, they will charge into it with teeth bared. A strike cruiser against a Gloriana-class battleship is an utter mismatch, even without whatever sorcery Verngar is working, but the Red Wolves clearly have no intention of dying on anything less than their own terms.

'The *Spectre of Ruin* is moving up astern!' the auspex officer calls.

'Forgemaster Valthex wishes to know if he should engage the *Wolf of Fenris!*' the vox-officer adds.

'I knew that granting him the command of your old ship was a good idea,' Verngar says to Huron with a smile. 'At least it seems that *some* warriors understand loyalty.'

'Lord Huron is correct, Verngar. Your actions are folly.'

That voice is not on the bridge: it comes from the vox. Huron recognises the grating tones of Captain Sargotta, never one not to speak her mind. Verngar throws a venomous glance at the vox-officer.

'Did you leave it on an open channel?'

'Yes, lord, forgive me, but you never said–'

This time Verngar's muttering is quicker and less complex, and it culminates in a flash of light from the Ebon Talon.

The vox-officer screams.

He stands up from his station, his body going rigid, and then his skin begins to crack. Brilliant light shines out from the hairlines that craze their way across him, as though he is being burned up from the inside out by something of ferocious heat. His eyes and mouth glow white for a moment before the screaming stops, his skins rapidly blackens into ash, and he crumbles to the deck.

Huron freezes in place. So, the artefact has power, destructive power at that, and Verngar has learned to harness it. The Hamadrya circles his shoulders, chittering half-words to him quietly.

The crewer next to the vox-officer's station reaches out and quietly deactivates the open channel.

'Status of the *Wolf of Fenris*?' Verngar snarls.

'Still approaching, lord,' comes the shaky reply. 'Should we launch torpedoes? Or come around to broadside them?'

'There is no need,' Verngar growls. 'I shall deal with them myself.'

It is quite a claim, but as the Apostate launches into his muttered chant once more, it seems obvious that Verngar believes he can back it up. Huron eyes the tactical hololith, assessing ranges and distances. Strike cruiser against battleship might nominally be a mismatch, but only if both sides are firing…

Huron feels the disturbance in the warp like a bow wave, and he knows what is coming.

'Warp signature!' the auspex officer calls. 'I'm detecting incoming warp jumps!'

'How many?' Huron demands.

'I…' The officer gestures helplessly to the readings. Huron glances at them and watches the numbers climb, as the cogitators of the *Macragge's Honour* calculate, and recalculate, and calculate again…

Then the translation begins.

The darkness shimmers, and capital ship after capital ship translates back into realspace. Huron casts his eyes over the idents that flash up: the *Light of Honour*, the *Glory of Ultramar*, the *Blade Defiant*, the *Calth's Fury*...

The *Macragge's Honour* knows these ships well.

'Guilliman's wretches!' Huron snarls. And still they come! They have translated in close; it has to be purest chance, but their vanguard is already in range of the flank of the Red Corsairs' fleet. Weapons fire begins to sparkle in the void, and the drawn-out dance of destruction starts anew.

'They cannot have responded to a distress signal from this planet!' the Apostate rages, rounding on Huron. 'There hasn't been the time!'

'And yet here they are, nonetheless,' Huron points out. 'Perhaps the forefront of their crusade was closer than we thought.' He spreads his hands. 'Well, *Lord* Verngar? This is your command, after all. Do we fight, or do we run?'

Running is the sensible option, so far as Huron can see. The Imperium has arrived in force that at least matches the Red Corsairs' fleet, and their angle of attack will punch into Verngar's flank before many of his ships can bring themselves around to properly meet the threat. Verngar had counted on the only resistance coming from within the Ogrys System, and now that lack of vision is coming back to bite him. Additionally, although they have not ransacked Ogrys as thoroughly as they would have liked, they have already secured valuable plunder. They would not be leaving empty-handed, and will have further damaged the Imperium's attempts to refortify this world.

However, the Apostate's blood is up, and Huron can see the desperate anger of a warrior who refuses to accept that what should have been an easy victory is slipping from his grasp.

'Broadside!' Verngar shouts. He still holds the Talon, but even he has realised that he has more pressing concerns than the mutinous Red Wolves. Despite the force deployed against them, the *Macragge's Honour* is still the mightiest ship here, and the newcomers are heading straight for it. 'Open fire at the closest target!'

'Guns are not responding!'

Verngar's head snaps around. 'What did you say?'

'The guns aren't responding, lord! They won't fire!'

Huron chuckles, and his wheezing rasp rolls out over the bridge. He gestures at the hololith, where shining dot after shining dot of Ultramarines ships are converging on the defenceless *Macragge's Honour*.

'I think they want their ship back, don't you, Verngar? And I am not convinced that the *Macragge's Honour* doesn't want that as well.' He smiles. 'I thought you said the machine-spirit was tractable?'

Verngar casts a venomous glance at Turazan, but the warpsmith has already extruded a mechatendril into the nearest data-port. However, his expression is grim.

'It is no use, Lord Verngar. The ship refuses to acknowledge Ultramarines vessels as enemies, and all ships within range are Ultramarines.'

'Have they fired yet?' Huron calls.

'No, lord!' the auspex officer confirms, with considerable relief in his tone.

'They're intending to board,' Huron tells Verngar. 'If those ships are carrying anywhere near their full complement, we're going to be overrun by close on two full companies of Ultramarines, including this new breed.' He shakes his head. 'Never fight when the opponent has chosen the ground. We should withdraw – we have achieved partial success, we can still hit

Chogoris, and the tides of the warp will be kinder to us than to them, even if they can somehow puzzle out our destination to follow us.'

Verngar's lip curls, but no matter how he glances from the hololith to the viewport and back again, he cannot change the reality of the situation. If the Apostate had been the sort of warrior who would always fight and die, he would have stayed in the Angels Encarmine and been executed as a heretic. It cuts him to the bone to do so, but he will not sit helpless and wait for the Ultramarines to come and take his head.

'Signal all ships!' he snarls. 'Translate immediately! Do not mention Chogoris – we must keep that knowledge from the Imperium!'

An enterprising crewer steps into the vox-officer's vacant station and opens a channel. The word is passed out: Verngar the Apostate is calling for the retreat.

Sirens begin to wail as the *Macragge's Honour* prepares to activate its Geller fields, engage its warp engines, and make the jump into the immaterium. However, new sirens start ringing, throwing a different note into the chaos of the bridge.

'Incoming fire!' someone shouts. 'The *Wolf of Fenris* has opened fire on us!'

Huron laughs: the Red Wolves are not ones to forget a threat made to them, even in the face of a new danger. Verngar, however, is not so amused, and he whirls around to check the hololith and see how long they have before impact, and to judge whether the shields can withstand the approaching attack.

Huron raises the Tyrant's Claw and triggers the heavy flamer.

The gout of flame rushes out and engulfs Verngar from behind, washing over him and clinging to his armour and his flesh. He bellows in pain and stumbles forwards, still clutching the Ebon Talon to his chest.

The two Possessed snarl as one, and leap for Huron, but they would have done well to heed their prior wariness of him. The Hamadrya whispers in his ear, and Huron summons the warp and bends it to his will with the speed of thought. It is no easy matter to tear a daemon out of a body once it has taken hold, but Huron has gained certain insights into the ways of the empyrean and its denizens.

Besides, even if such an endeavour does not succeed, it is still *extremely* painful for the subject.

Verngar's bodyguards collapse onto the deck, shrieking in agony as spirit and flesh are prised apart, and unnatural forms sustained by daemonic energy become fully beholden to the laws of physics once more. Huron does not wait to see the outcome: he activates his power axe and beheads the first, then simply pulverises the skull of the second with a blow from the Tyrant's Claw.

Fire. Fire in his heart.

Verngar is back on his feet, and the Ebon Talon is glowing in his hands even as the last of the flames still flicker over him. His armour is charred and partially melted, and his face is no longer the noble, undamaged visage of a son of Sanguinius, but he can still call upon the power of the artefact.

Had Verngar not already done this in front of him once, Huron might have succumbed. The Hamadrya is a fast learner, however, and it guides Huron's mind to the source of the power.

For a moment, the pain inside him builds until he feels he is about to explode. Then the pathway opens for him to redirect it, and over at the data-port, Warpsmith Turazan stiffens and begins to scream as glowing cracks spread across his skin.

'He has reaped the consequences,' Huron tells Verngar breathlessly. He feels as though just touching that power for a second has hollowed him out completely, but he is still on his feet. He is not dead yet, and from the look on Verngar's face, the Apostate has realised that his prized artefact cannot be trusted to prevail against the Blood Reaver.

Verngar snatches Stormfiend from where it is mag-clamped to his back, and activates it with a crackle of power. He rushes at Huron, an Adeptus Astartes in his prime charging an old, broken-down warrior. Verngar has the advantage of strength, and speed, and fury.

Huron has the advantage of always being in just the wrong place for his enemy's blows to land. He reaches up with the Tyrant's Claw to catch the thunder hammer on its downswing, and begins to bring his power axe around to bury it in Verngar's breastplate.

But Verngar's hammer is not where it should be, and it is Huron's breastplate that takes the first impact.

The stored energy is released with a deafening *crack*, and Huron is propelled backwards across the bridge by the force of the blow, colliding with the base of Guilliman's throne. The back of his head splits open and he blinks, trying to clear his vision, but there are still two Verngars rushing towards him. That does not mean he has lost track of his countdown, though.

Three…

He raises the Tyrant's Claw and fires again, on the basis that precision is hardly needed.

Two…

Both Apostates roll under the bloom of flame, and come up standing over Huron with Stormfiend raised. Huron tumbles desperately aside from the blow, which shatters the steps where he had been lying, but Verngar follows him with a howl of fury and prepares another strike.

One…

The *Macragge's Honour* rocks slightly as its shields take the full force of the salvo from the *Wolf of Fenris*. The mighty battleship is still undamaged, but Verngar is distracted for a moment as the sirens hit a new pitch, and the viewports light up with electromagnetic flares.

Huron kicks out, and takes his enemy's legs from under him.

Verngar falls, and hits the deck with a tumultuous clatter of ceramite. Huron reaches out with the Tyrant's Claw, but Verngar has no wish to taste the weapon again at point-blank range, and he drops Stormfiend to force the mighty power claw upwards and away from his face. Huron activates the power field and Verngar's gauntlet begins to smoke and sizzle. Huron uses his enemy's grip to lever himself back to his feet, and as Verngar's hand begins to disintegrate, the Blood Reaver has the high ground once more.

Huron, standing over Verngar, triggers the flamer again.

The Apostate takes the full force of it, and screams and thrashes. He is still a Space Marine, and so he still has the resolve and the strength to roll over and begin to crawl away, but Huron brings his power axe down onto the Apostate's backpack power unit. Sparks fly, and Verngar's movements become weaker, and more laboured.

He still clings to the Ebon Talon with his remaining hand. Huron severs it at the wrist, then picks it up. He does not touch the Talon itself, even with his armoured hand. He has seen Verngar's reaction to it, and Huron Blackheart has no wish to be caught by ties the nature of which he does not yet even know.

He activates his vox. 'Valthex.'

'Lord Huron?'

'Do it.'

Huron stares down at the ruined but still-living form of Verngar the Apostate. He feels he should smile, but he no longer has the energy. 'Please give the Ultramarines my regards, when they arrive.'

The bridge begins to turn grey, and then *something* hooks around Huron's heart, and yanks him apart.

EIGHTEEN

Cybernetica Datasmith Griza Dallax hears the warning klaxons begin to wail. The *Macragge's Honour* is preparing to jump into the warp, even though they surely cannot have already finished their plundering of the world they are attacking. She connects to a data-port, and vocalises the binharic equivalent of a sigh of relief at what she encounters. The machine-spirit of this ancient, mighty vessel is still strong, and although there are threads of scrapcode running through its hallowed systems, accessing it is nothing like the flood of caustic filth to which she exposed herself the only time she tried this on the *Spectre of Ruin*.

She checks. Yes, the ship's systems are showing multiple contacts of other Ultramarines vessels, approaching fast. What is more, rogue elements within the ship have emerged, as the arrival of their former masters encourages the survivors of the *Macragge's Honour*'s original crew to rise up. Events are unfolding exactly as Huron Blackheart told her they would. Against all reasonable calculations, it seems that the Blood Reaver has been true to his word.

Now it is time for Griza Dallax to be true to hers: not for the sake of Huron, but for the good of the Imperium. On this one issue, it appears that Huron's interests, the Imperium's and hers all converge.

Griza sends a blurt of command code to her remaining three kastelans, who respond immediately. She wastes half a second blink-clicking picts of them. No matter the outcome of this, she will likely never see them again. She has detected no fewer than twenty-seven minor deviations in form and programming across the trio; even without the direct attentions of any of the Red Corsairs' hereteks, the exposure to the warp has begun to change their forms, their very machine-spirits. Dallax is not aware of any such alterations in herself, but she suspects they are there, perhaps taking some form that conceals them from her own diagnostics. She will very likely no longer have any place in the Adeptus Mechanicus, and that means she probably has no future at all.

But that will not matter, if she can accomplish one final function.

The corridors of the *Macragge's Honour* have acquired a tarnish since it has been in the possession of the Red Corsairs: a layer of filth and grime and old blood, and the lingering hints of putrefaction. However, the superstructure and interior of the vessel have not warped in any meaningful way, and there are no unexpected dead ends or false turns, let alone hungry darknesses where the walls will devour the unwary. Dallax hastens towards her destination, reaching it in under a minute. She is not challenged, because everyone on board has their own concerns; and besides, who on a Red Corsairs vessel is going to challenge a tech-priest accompanied by three heavily armed battle automata? Only someone who is confident that they will not get obliterated for their temerity, and there are none of those here – merely harried crewers with scarred and branded flesh, wearing the sigils of foul gods.

Dallax reaches the doors of the enginarium, and activates the opening mechanism. It is, theoretically, locked, but she can find her way around the security protocols, and the *Macragge's Honour* provides her with no more than a perfunctory obstacle. Dallax wonders if it can sense that she, like itself, has not yet completely fallen into darkness; that she, like itself, yet has a role to play in the service of the Omnissiah.

The doors grind open, revealing the mighty chamber in which are housed the warp engines. Dallax steps through, and into a realm of wonders and horror.

The ancient machinery that has moved this battleship between the warp and realspace for over ten millennia is a marvel of technology, and it has been defaced. The symbol of the Mechanicus has been torn down and replaced by a skull that leers out from an eight-pointed star, and the cables that connect the towering machines of the engine itself now drip with ichor and tainted liquids. All around her, the floor and the walls are covered with glyphs that combine mathematical formulae with entreaties to dark powers: glyphs that hurt her optical sensors, even though it should technically be impossible for her to register any physical sensation from the lenses that now serve as her eyes. The air is heavy with the scent of corrosion, and she can taste static on her tongue.

None of that is as important as the fact that three robed adepts of the Dark Mechanicum are turning towards her, interrupted from the ritual with which they had been about to activate the machinery around them. Beyond them, Dallax sees a dozen or so cult followers, wretches who live only to serve their foul masters, and to debase the creations of the Omnissiah.

<Interrogative: who are you?> the closest adept snarls, the code of his floodstream so corrupted that it causes a spasm in the left side of Dallax's body, not to mention rendering him nearly unintelligible to her.

But she is not here to make conversation.

She raises her gamma pistol and shoots him. He howls as he burns, but that is the only free shot she is going to get: the other two hereteks erupt into a twisted nightmare of weaponry and other, fouler tools, and send scrapcode sleeting towards her to overwhelm her cogitators.

The kastelans open up, their heavy phosphor blasters engulfing the dark tech-priests in blinding white fire, but after only a second or so they switch targets. Not to the onrushing cultists – they are unimportant – but to the sacred machinery of the warp drives themselves.

Griza Dallax has thought herself long past the human notion of a breaking heart, but the dispassionate analysis of her own experiences, even as she shoots down more hereteks, confirms to her that she is experiencing symptoms that match the recorded physiological signs of grief. Resisting the urge to order her charges to stop their vandalism is the hardest thing she has ever done, but she hardens herself to it. She might die, and her automata may be destroyed, but if enough damage is done quickly enough, then there is no power in this galaxy or outside it that will allow the followers of the Dark Mechanicum to drag this ship into the warp.

One of the adepts lunges towards her, half-melted from phosphor fire, but still ferocious and deadly. Dallax plunges the energised fingers of her power fist into his chest before he can react, and tears out everything within her grasp. Even the boons of the heretekal cannot grant him the ability to survive such trauma, and he collapses with a feeble blurt of binharic cursing.

Dallax aims for the next one. She does not know for sure what Huron Blackheart's plan is; all she knows is that she has the chance to strand the *Macragge's Honour* here long enough for the Imperium to recover it.

She has asked herself whether she should be aiding such a deadly foe of the Imperium in this manner, even if he is offering her the opportunity of redemption, but she has decided that she must act on the data available to her. It is possible that if she refused Huron's bargain, or betrayed him once it was made, the Imperium would benefit through a scheme of his being foiled, but she has no way of knowing if that would be the case. What she *can* be reasonably sure of is that the Ultramarines recovering their primarch's flagship, and its resources being denied to the Red Corsairs, is a tangible benefit. One worth giving her life for.

As the cultists close in, too many to shoot down before they reach her, Griza Dallax commends her motive force to the Omnissiah, and prepares to buy her charges as much time as possible.

NINETEEN

He is adrift in static, lost in moments that last for lifetimes. He is everywhere and nowhere. He is being pushed face first through a wall of grey knives. His tendons are aflame, his bones are ice. In this place, at this moment, his body is whole once again, and all of it hurts.

And there are the voices.

Huron.

Huron.

HURON.

He ignores them, even though their touch lingers on him, even though their claws snag on his flesh and their barbs burrow in towards his marrow. This is eternity, but he will stare eternity in the face and dare it to blink first.

He is Lugft Huron, Huron Blackheart, the Tyrant of Badab and the Blood Reaver, traitor, heretic and outcast warlord, and he is too stubborn to die.

* * *

Huron collapses onto the floor of the *Spectre of Ruin*'s teleportarium, and sucks breath back into lungs that feel more starved of oxygen than those of a Space Marine should. His armour is smoking with the after-effects of being dragged through the warp. Commonly held wisdom is that only those within Terminator armour can be teleported effectively, let alone survive it, but Huron can swim in deeper currents of the warp than can most mortals, and he has done this before. It usually requires ferocious concentration, and sometimes leaves him somewhat drained.

This time it almost killed him. But 'almost' is good enough.

'Lord!' Armenneus Valthex exclaims, starting forward. Huron accepts the assistance offered by the Alchemancer to get him back to his feet. He trusts Valthex, as much as he trusts anyone. Valthex saw Huron on the verge of death a century ago, and assisted him away from it at the cost of considerable effort and personal risk. If he were to betray Huron now, it would feel more like a debt being called in than anything else.

Valthex does no such thing, and Huron makes it upright again with the Alchemancer's help. He hands Valthex the Ebon Talon, still clutched in Verngar's severed hand.

'Study it,' Huron rasps, his voice even more strained than usual. 'I want to know everything we can about it. I know it has power, but I am not going to rush blindly into using it – I saw the effect it was already having on Verngar. And don't touch it with your own hands,' he adds.

Valthex nods, and extends a mechatendril to pluck it from Huron's grasp. 'I will report my findings directly to you, lord.'

'But first, get us into the warp and away from here,' Huron says.

'We were already at readiness, and I gave the order as soon as you materialised,' Valthex assures him. Sure enough, Huron feels his flagship shudder, and then the ice-water sensation down his skeleton that informs him he has once more slipped into the warp, although this time it is within the protection of a Geller field, and the voices that plagued him should have no way of reaching him, at least for a while.

They will be back, whispering threats and entreaties in what would be the same breath, if they needed to breathe. He will wall them out again, unless and until he has need of them. If he has his way, that day will be a long time coming.

'Should we expect further problems from the Apostate?' Valthex asks, looking meaningfully at the severed hand held in his mechatendril.

'I doubt it,' Huron says, with a breathy chuckle. 'He was mostly dead when I left him, and I doubt the Ultramarines will be interested in keeping him alive. As for other problems he could cause us – even if they interrogate him and he tells them that we are destined for Chogoris, they'll have no reason to assume he's not lying to them with his dying breaths.'

'The *Macragge's Honour* won't translate?' Valthex asks. 'They were activating Geller fields and warp drives.'

Huron shakes his head. 'I doubt they'll make it. And it will be no great loss to us – the machine-spirit is clearly still unreliable. Let the Ultramarines busy themselves for the next decade "cleansing" it of our presence. In truth, I find the notion somewhat amusing.'

'I see.' Valthex's expression suggests that he does not, but that he is not going to question his lord too closely. 'But how do we know that Guilliman's whelps will not be able to divine our next target? After all, they must have been forewarned of our attack on Ogrys somehow. The chances of such a fleet happening to be so close to the system as to come to its aid in that short a time are astronomically small.'

'They won't know our next target, because this time, I haven't told them,' Huron replies. He smiles wearily at Valthex's expression. 'Never fight a battle on ground of your opponent's choosing, Valthex. Verngar faced a sterner test than he anticipated, and his failings were exposed.' He chuckles. 'I did tell you not to lecture me on matters of warfare. And I told you not to disturb me in my chambers – it takes a considerable amount of effort to project an astropathic message when you are not one of the Emperor's worms who specialise in such things, and even more to prevent those who receive it from realising your identity. Had the ritual been interrupted, the consequences for both of us could have been… unpleasant.'

Valthex nods slowly. If he disapproves of Huron's gambit, he is possessed of greater sense than to say so. 'So this bargain you spoke of. It was to allow you to reach across the warp?'

'Oh no.' Huron shakes his head. 'I could do that myself, although as I said, not without considerable effort. No, the bargain I spoke of was rather more mundane, and yet, I believe, no less effective.' He pauses. 'And it was made with someone to whom I feel I owed a favour.'

He straightens. His body is singing its song of pain to him, but he knows this tune. It is time to make someone else dance to it.

'Let us go and drench the world of the White Scars in blood and make mountains from their corpses, until they realise that their Emperor is truly dead, and Guilliman is nothing but the desperate, doomed last hope of an Imperium built on lies.'

'And what of Abaddon, lord?' Valthex enquires.

Huron sighs. 'What of him? We are bringing death to the Imperium – he can hardly take issue with that. And if he does…'

Huron smiles.

'A Warmaster has fallen before, Valthex. It can happen again.'

ACKNOWLEDGEMENTS

This was the first novel I wrote while in lockdown, so the first thanks must go to my wife, Janine, who is by far the best person with whom I could hope to be essentially confined to a single house for an extended period of time.

Secondly, thanks go to Benji, Jos, Julie, Nick and Spike, for our regular online game sessions. About the only thing I'll miss about this pandemic when we get more active social lives again is back-stabbing you all on a more-or-less weekly basis, even if it's been via a computer screen rather than in person around a table ('Not with that attitude, you won't!').

Thirdly, I would like to extend my thanks to the other authors who have written Huron before me, such as Graham McNeill and Sarah Cawkwell, and in particular Aaron Dembski-Bowden. Aaron's *Night Lords* trilogy was a wonderful insight into how to make 'modern day' Chaos Space Marines interesting and compelling, and although Huron was a secondary character in those books, it was that portrayal's bile and spite – and the sensation that he might be closer to death than life, but he can still at any moment send you there before him – that I most wanted to harness for this novel.

I would also, of course, like to thank Will Moss at Black Library for allowing me to have so much fun with this, and his guidance and advice. Even if he did prevent me from having Huron quote the Rock. But I guess that's what he's for.

And finally, thanks to everyone who's read this, and indeed any of my other work for Black Library. Having been a Games Workshop player for thirty years, it's still an incredible thrill to *get paid to write stories* about the things I used to gawk at on the shelves of the store in Ipswich Debenhams. Thank you for giving me the chance to continue doing so.

ABOUT THE AUTHOR

Mike Brooks is a science fiction and fantasy author who lives in Nottingham. His recent work for Black Library includes the Warhammer 40,000 novels *Warboss*, *Brutal Kunnin*, *Da Big Dakka*, *Harrowmaster*, *Huron Blackheart: Master of the Maelstrom* and *The Lion: Son of the Forest.* He has also written the Horus Heresy Primarchs novel *Alpharius: Head of the Hydra*, the Necromunda titles *Road to Redemption* and *Wanted: Dead*, and the Warhammer 40,000 titles *Rites of Passage* and *Da Gobbo's Revenge*. When not writing, he plays guitar and sings in a punk band, and DJs wherever anyone will tolerate him.

MORE FROM BLACK LIBRARY

FULGRIM: THE PERFECT SON
by Jude Reid

For too long the Emperor's Children have been denied their birthright. Their once-glorious Legion has been fractured into disparate warbands, condemned to ravage world after futile world in the pursuit of ambition and excess. But no longer.

For these stories and more, go to **blacklibrary.com**, **warhammer.com**, Games Workshop and Warhammer stores, all good book stores or visit one of the thousands of independent retailers worldwide, which can be found at **warhammer.com/store-finder**

MORE FROM BLACK LIBRARY

THE LION: SON OF THE FOREST
by Mike Brooks

The Lion. Son of the Emperor, brother of demigods and primarch of the Dark Angels. Awakened. Returned. And yet… lost.

For these stories and more, go to **blacklibrary.com**, **warhammer.com**, Games Workshop and Warhammer stores, all good book stores or visit one of the thousands of independent retailers worldwide, which can be found at **warhammer.com/store-finder**

MORE FROM BLACK LIBRARY

GHAZGHKULL THRAKA: PROPHET OF THE WAAAGH!
by Nate Crowley

Ghazghkull Thraka, the Beast of Armageddon, is one of the greatest threats to the Imperium. For the first time, read his full story… as told to the Inquisition by his faithful banner bearer Makari.

For these stories and more, go to **blacklibrary.com**, **warhammer.com**, Games Workshop and Warhammer stores, all good book stores or visit one of the thousands of independent retailers worldwide, which can be found at **warhammer.com/store-finder**